This Is Ellen Jones Reporting

ISBN 978-1-7366448-0-5

Editing & Publishing Services
www.yourextraordinarybook.com

Author Website
www.alaynesmith.com

This Is Ellen Jones Reporting

ALAYNE SMITH

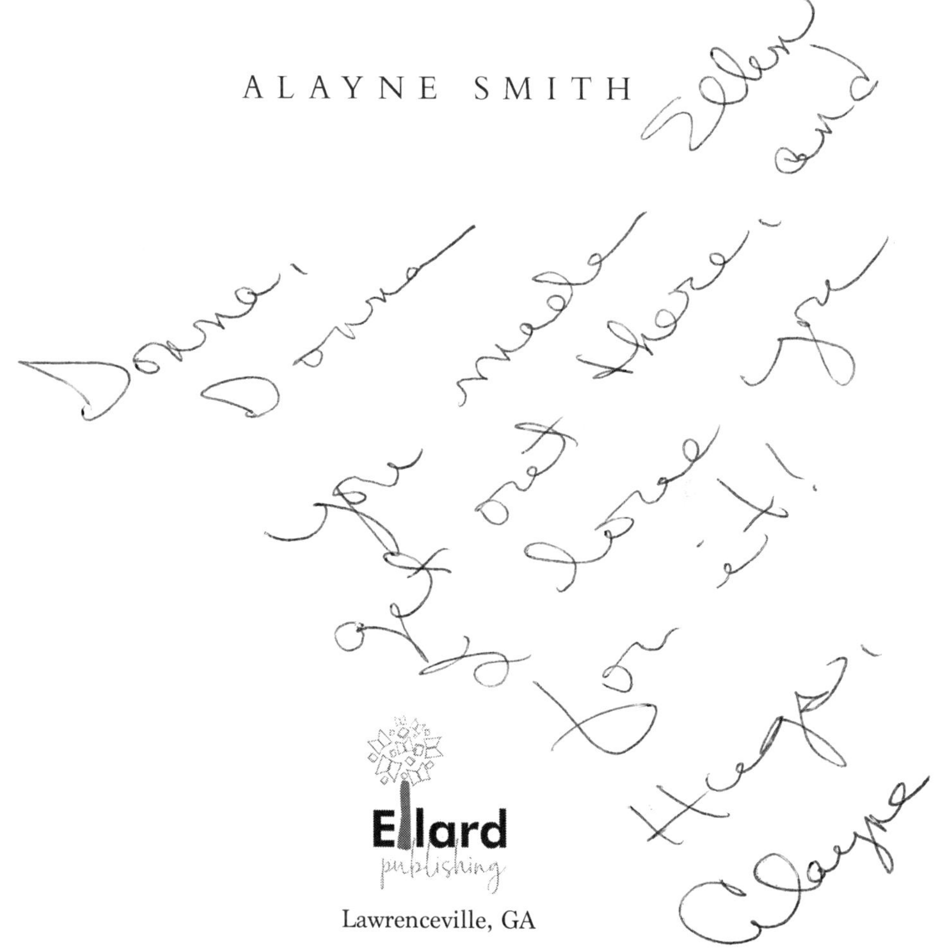

Ellard

publishing

Lawrenceville, GA

CONTENTS

Chapter One: Luke and Ellen — 1

Chapter Two: The First Stand-Upper — 7

Chapter Three: Aunt Zia — 13

Chapter Four: Amelia — 17

Chapter Five: A Call from Home — 23

Chapter Six: Jo Jo — 27

Chapter Seven: A Newscast Meeting — 33

Chapter Eight: Adventures With Amelia — 38

Chapter Nine: The Merrick House Robbery — 43

Chapter Ten: Jo Jo Goes Downtown — 49

Chapter Eleven: Ellen And Luke — 53

Chapter Twelve: Ellen's Family Comes To Miami — 59

Chapter Thirteen: Mr. Chenard — 67

Chapter Fourteen: Hoyt V. Florida — 77

Chapter Fifteen: The Ladies Of Libya — 81

Chapter Sixteen: Mr. Chenard — 85

Chapter Seventeen: Hide Your Panties — 91

Chapter Eighteen: Luke And Ellen — 97

Chapter Nineteen: Ellen Goes Home — 101

Chapter Twenty: Brigade 2506 — 109

Chapter Twenty-One: Thanksgiving Day — 117

Chapter Twenty-Two: Ellen And Julio — 125

Chapter Twenty-Three: Jo Jo And Ilenia — 131

Chapter Twenty-Four: Luke And Sandra — 137

Chapter Twenty-Five: Mr. Chenard — 145

Chapter Twenty-Six: Ellen Directs — 149

Chapter Twenty-Seven: Ellen Meets Luke's Parents — 153

Chapter Twenty-Eight: A Piña Colada Salad — 159

Chapter Twenty-Nine: Carlota — 165

Chapter Thirty: A Letter From Jo Jo — 169

Chapter Thirty-One: The Peabody Award Story — 173

Chapter Thirty-Two: A Cuban Party — 179

Chapter Thirty-Three: Ellen Talks To Dr. Shelby — 185

Chapter Thirty-Four: Christmas In Alabama — 189

Chapter Thirty-Five: Carlota's Memorial Service — 199

Chapter Thirty-Six: Ellen Says Goodbye To Luke — 209

Chapter Thirty-Seven: A Letter From Jo Jo — 213

Chapter Thirty-Nine: This Is Ellen Jones Reporting — 217

ELLEN'S NOTEBOOK

Lighting — 221

Hard News Story Forms — 223

Editing Rules — 225

Jo Jo's Letter: Travel Photo Album — 227

Jo Jo's Letter: Travel Photo Album — 231

Mr. Chenard: Travel Photo Album — 233

Jo Jo And Ilenia: Travel Photo Album — 238

A Letter From Jo Jo: Travel Photo Album — 239

Acknowledgments — 243

About the Author — 247

OCTOBER 1961

Luke and Ellen

Walking out of the movie theater in Miami—the one closest to the university campus—Luke pulls Ellen closer to him. They've just seen *Breakfast at Tiffany's,* and Ellen is still musing on why Holly Golightly made the decisions she made. Purposeful, high-reaching Ellen can't quite understand the erratic and capricious Holly.

"Lighten up, Ellen. It's a movie." Without another word, Luke jumps up on a sidewalk bench and belts out "Moon River."

Ellen watches this larger-than-life man she loves as he sings, gesturing with his arms as an accompaniment to the lyrics. Paul Newman? Is there a little Paul Newman in Luke? He's a gorgeous man with his blue eyes, square jaw, and dark hair that coils along his neck. He is lean and glides along the bench like he owns the space around him.

Ellen and Luke are broadcast journalism majors at the University of Columbus in Miami. He's a senior to Ellen's junior. Luke is an anchor on the daily news show aired by the department. So far Ellen has been behind the scenes. She's challenging herself to be in front of the camera this year.

Watching Luke, Ellen remembers the day she told him she loved him. It was the perfect setting, so romantic—a wedding on the wide porch of Callander, her grandfather's antebellum home. The wedding party was stationed on the porch, awaiting the bride. The men on the plantation had moved the grand piano from the front parlor to the porch and, as the pianist played Wagner's "Bridal Chorus" from *Lohengrin*, the bride passed through Callander's eight-foot-tall double front doors onto the porch. Ellen, the maid of honor, could hear the gasp of the crowd watching from the front lawn.

After Amanda and Will complete the vows, Ellen sees Luke at the back of the crowd. Luke smiles at her. How strange to see Luke from her college life here among her Alabama family and friends. It's the first time she has seen him in a suit and tie, and she watches him as he moves with ease, making his way through the crowd toward the porch. As Luke walks with confidence up the steps of the wide porch, the strong Ellen, who shows so little emotion, finds herself trembling.

The crowd moves into the ballroom, and Luke and Ellen flow with them. As the orchestra plays "When I Fall in Love," Luke takes her in his arms, and, as they dance, Ellen feels the strongest love for this handsome, self-assured, sometimes irritating man. Luke's been waiting months for Ellen to tell him she loves him. In this setting, on the perfect spring day, Ellen looks Luke in the eye and says, "I love you." Somehow, it fits that she and Luke are together at this time and place. She loves him.

But she hated him first. Last year, when Ellen volunteered at the J building, the broadcast journalism building where the head of the department, Dr. Shelby, let her run camera during the daily news show, there was no love lost between Ellen and the brash Luke. Ellen could not officially be in the broadcast department until her junior year. Luke, the male anchor, called himself "Luke the legend." What an egotist! Ellen hated his arrogance. She hated that he called her "Maid of Cotton." She despised him for his condescending attitude. And she kept despising him until the night he asked for a dance, then helped her with her Aunt Zia, and one day told her that he loved her.

Luke finishes "Moon River" and jumps down from the bench. "Hey, Cotton. Wanna hear about tomorrow's lead? Roger Maris—you know he's with the Yankees—hit his sixty-first home run in the last game of the season. They were playing the Red Sox."

"This is the lead story?" Ellen says, skepticism in her voice.

"Well, yes, sugar. Roger Maris beat the thirty-four-year-old record held by Babe Ruth. Now, what about you? What are you working on?"

"I'm finally going to be on-air. I'm reporting on President Kennedy advising U.S. families to build bomb shelters."

"I missed that story. It came through on the AP wire?"

"Yes. The President is advising families to protect themselves from atomic fallout in case we have a nuclear exchange with the Soviet Union. If the Soviets attack, the lives of Americans not directly hit in the blast can be saved if they take shelter and stay there."

"Oh, bull. We can't go around worrying about this."

"Luke, you have to realize... President Kennedy has to take precautions. The Soviets conducted thirty nuclear tests this year alone."

"Look, I know it's a real situation, and we have to report it. Just saying we can't live our lives constantly in fear. We can't make all our decisions based on this threat. Think, Cotton. Will you stop planning our wedding because of a possible nuclear explosion in our country?"

"Luke, you're taking this to extremes. Of course, we go on with our lives. But it's a threat, and we'd be insane not to prepare."

"Okay, okay. You and the President are right. Now, speaking of our wedding, when do you think we should have the wedding? I'm guessing the where is a given. Callander."

"Yes. I want to be married at Callander. I don't know when. Should I graduate before we marry? That's almost two years."

"Gee, Ellen. We can't wait that long. How about this summer, after I graduate?"

"But, I'll have another year of school."

"Yes, and even though I'm determined to work in New York, I probably won't right away. So, unless I get lucky, I'll probably work somewhere else. It has got to be a major market, though. I'm only going to work in a major market like Chicago, Boston, or Los Angeles. I wouldn't mind working at WGN-TV in Chicago. You know it was one of the first television stations to broadcast live in color? So, what do ya think? Do you see us living in the Windy City, Cotton? We could go to the Navy Pier and Soldier Field!

Or Boston, maybe. You love history. Imagine seeing the Boston Harbor where the Sons of Liberty dumped tea in the harbor. And we could certainly live in Los Angeles. It would be a dream come true for me to work with Jerry Dunphy."

"And who is Jerry Dunphy?"

"Cotton, you amaze me. How could you not know Jerry Dunphy?

He and some others at CBS started the 'Big News' concept of televising the news. He only set the standard for news all over our country."

"Slow down, Luke. I'll still have another year of school."

"We'll work it out, Ellen. I want you with me. Selfish, I know."

Luke reaches over and takes Ellen's hand as they walk toward her dorm. Silence. No sound but their footsteps falling on October leaves scattered along the cobblestone sidewalk. Ellen is imagining what life might be like with Luke. *Will his career always come first? Can she live with that—forever molding her own career to fit in with Luke's?*

Luke senses she's troubled. When they get to her dorm, Caldwell Hall, Luke turns Ellen toward him and folds her in his arms. "Don't worry, Ellen. We'll work it all out—the wedding, our jobs, our lives. I love you. It's going to be a wonderful life!"

Ellen bends Luke's neck down to kiss him. "I know, Luke. It is going to be a wonderful life for the two of us."

She turns to walk up the steps to Caldwell, a brick affair with the character so often found in buildings that have stood for more than a hundred years. Caldwell has a central section flanked with wings on each side, with column-lined front porches that run from side to side across the length of the building. But it's the main section that Ellen falls in love with every time she walks through the rich mahogany front doors. Three columned arches form the front entrance, and bougainvillea almost completely covers them. Inside the arches, three mahogany doors topped with semicircular transom lights that look something like glass fans add to the romance of the historic building that is her college home.

Inside the lobby, Ellen walks down the right wing to her dorm room, a room with a window onto the front porch—a front porch that provides easy access to Ellen's room. She's barely entered the room when she hears a tapping on her window. She knows it's Luke: he's done this before.

Brushing aside the long drapery, Ellen watches as Luke pantomimes the words, "I love you." Ellen tugs at the iron window handle until the mammoth window slides upwards.

"Come here, you," Ellen says as she pulls Luke toward her.

Ellen flops down on her bed. Okay, this is a problem. Ellen doesn't believe in human sacrifice. Why should she sacrifice a career for marriage? But Ellen loves Luke. She wants to support him. To marry him. To be at his side. To have him by her side.

Ellen comes from generations of women who stayed at home, "keeping house" while their husbands worked outside the home. World War II changed everything. Men were off fighting, and someone had to fill the job vacancies they left behind. That would be the women. After the war, women weren't necessarily content to go back to ironing, cooking, and sweeping. They had a taste of working for pay, and they liked it. And the country needed secretaries, teachers, and nurses.

But not for Ellen. For as long as she can remember, she has wanted to be a broadcast journalist like her Aunt Zia. Ellen doesn't know how she and Luke will work out having careers and a marriage. Could she ever give up her career to follow Luke?

The First Stand-Upper

Dr. Shelby, head of the broadcast journalism department, is lecturing Ellen's class about the Peabody Awards. Dr. Shelby requires all broadcast journalism juniors and seniors to submit an entry.

"The Peabody was established in 1938 by the National Association of Broadcasters and is comparable to the Pulitzer. The award is named for George Foster Peabody, a philanthropist who wanted to improve education in the South. Oddly, he was friends with Franklin Delano Roosevelt and recommended that Roosevelt have a home in Warm Springs, Georgia. He thought the warm waters there would help Roosevelt, who suffered from paralysis.

The early years of the Peabody Awards consisted of awards in radio only; awards for televisions were first given in 1948. The Grady School of Journalism at the University of Georgia oversees the Peabody Awards. Programs from CBS and NBC won last year. The Peabody Awards to be awarded in March 1962 are for stories aired between January 1, 1961, and December 31, 1961. The bottom line is this: the Peabody recognizes excellence in broadcast journalism.

For students at Columbus, there are two categories you may consider—news stories or documentaries. Submissions open in mid-

October. Not a lot of time before Christmas.

Now, back to our shows. Ellen, I believe you have a stand-upper?"

"Yes, sir. It's my first."

"We'll film you on the library steps," says Dr. Shelby, who is observing Ellen fidgeting with her notes. "You aren't nervous, are you?"

"I am," replies Ellen. "I know the rules: always look into the camera lens, speak slowly and distinctly, and, if I mess up, keep going."

"You'll do fine, Ellen." Pensive, he looks down at the copy Ellen has provided for her debut in front of the camera. "I notice this sentence, 'The government will soon be protecting every American.' What exactly does President Kennedy mean by this statement?"

"The president is referring to designating buildings as fallout shelters, which will be marked and stocked with water and food. President Kennedy wants the American public to know that the government will work toward protecting all Americans."

"Good. Include that in your script. That's important information."

Ellen's eyes have strayed to the anchor's desk where Luke is working with the new anchor, Sandra Rowen. Sandra looks like the movie star Jennifer Jones with her cloud of dark hair and long fingernails, glistening with red polish. She's arguing with Luke. Good. Maybe Luke has met his match.

Noticing where Ellen is looking, Dr. Shelby remarks, "Ellen, I think our new anchor can hold her own with Luke. Have you met Sandra?"

"No, not yet. I hear she's from a television family."

"That's right. Sandra's father is with ABC in New York. Not an anchor, though. I think he's a director for the news show. Anyway, back to your stand-upper. We'll be using a boom microphone. Ray will be holding it. That's one less thing for you to worry about, no hand-held mic."

"I just need to remember my script."

"Stop worrying! Here's the rest of your crew—cameraman, Johnny, and our lighting expert, Sam. They're ready for you now."

"Okay, Dr. Shelby. I won't let you down."

Ellen follows the crew out of the studio, again noticing Luke and Sandra though she's trying not to notice. Luke throws his head back and laughs uproariously. There's something about the scene that bothers her. Maybe it's the fact that Luke seems so comfortable with Sandra now. Or that Sandra is perched on the edge of the desk watching Luke with seeming adoration. Sandra is sensuous, red fingernails and all. Ellen looks down at her own nails, bitten to the quick.

Once Ellen and her crew reach the library steps, Johnny explains the lighting and tells her why he's positioning her with the sun falling on the left side of her face.

"Okay, Ellen. A quick lesson in lighting. Whether shooting in the studio or the field, the lighting crew will set up a triangular lighting plan. The strongest light hitting the subject is the key light. We always position the key light on the left or right side of the subject at approximately a forty-five-degree angle," he says.

"And the sun is the key light in our shooting, right?" asks Ellen.

"Gold star, lady. Yes, the sun is the key light, and it's falling on the left side of your face. We need to add a fill light at a forty-five-degree angle on the right side of your face. For today's story, we're using a reflector as the fill light. A reflector can be something as simple as a piece of white poster board, but today we are using a professional reflector. Sam will be holding the reflector so that the light fills in the shadows on the right side of your face."

"And the third light?"

"It's the backlight and it is used to separate the actor from the background. I'm positioning it directly behind you. Now, we're ready to shoot."

Countdown from Johnny, "5, 4, 3." Then, silently with his fingers, 2, 1. Looking directly into the camera lens, Ellen begins.

Yesterday, in a speech from the Oval Office, President Kennedy addressed the nation on civil defense issues. The President encouraged citizens to build bomb shelters to protect themselves from radioactive fallout in the event of a nuclear explosion.

This is not the first time President Kennedy has encouraged United States citizens to build bomb shelters. After the Soviets imposed a blockade on West Berlin in 1948, the President advised in televised a nationwide speech that if a nuclear attack occurred, lives of citizens not hit in the blast could be saved if shelters were available and if citizens are warned in time to go to a shelter.

The Soviet Union and the United States, while allies during World War II, are now in the middle of the Cold War. Khrushchev, leader of the Soviet Union, has renewed open-air nuclear testing. Kennedy has promised to stand firm against communism and to strengthen American military forces.

Pause. Ellen freezes. *What's the rest of the story? Oh, no! Yes, yes. I remember.*

President Kennedy has assured citizens that the government would do its part by marking public buildings as fallout shelters.

Once again, President Kennedy has encouraged citizens of the United States to build bomb shelters as protection from a nuclear attack from the Soviet Union.

Ellen tags the story. "This is Ellen Jones reporting for *Miami News Now.*"

Waiting until she's sure she's off-air, Ellen slaps her open hand against her forehead.

"I paused Johnny, I paused. Drat."

"Ellen, it's fine. The viewers only hear your story once. A pause is not bad; it lets the viewer absorb the lead."

"But did I look frozen?"

"No, you did not. Come on. Let's go back to the studio."

"How did it go, Ellen?" asks Dr. Shelby.

"She did fine," says Johnny. "She paused in the middle of the story, but I liked the pause. Gives the viewer time to absorb the story. Ellen's worried…"

"I *am* worried," says Ellen. "For a minute there, I forgot the script."

"Well, we'll take a look at it when it's developed. It's probably just fine. The first story under your belt. I'm proud of you," says Dr. Shelby.

While Dr. Shelby is talking, Ellen notices Sandra again. She is giving Luke a smug look. A condescending look. As if to say, *What a baby! Not like us professionals.*

Thank heavens, Luke walks away from Sandra. He's coming toward Ellen. "Cotton, I predict you killed it. Stop worrying. Let's go get a coffee to celebrate."

Ellen appreciates Dr. Shelby's encouragement and Johnny's support. But it's Luke's approval she craves most of all.

Ellen looks back over her shoulder at Sandra as she leaves the studio with Luke. There's no mistaking it. A frown replaces Sandra's smug look.

Learn more about lighting in Ellen's Notebook at the end of this book.

Aunt Zia

Ellen walks into her empty dorm room, glad to be alone at the end of the day. Her eyes wander around the room and light on the family pictures grouped together on her student desk. Her father standing by his latest car. A shot of the Callander plantation house. Aunt Zia. Ellen picks up the photo of her Aunt Zia.

Aunt Zia has always been the one Ellen turns to with her problems. Not her own mother. Ellen loved her mother, Charlene, who took care of everyone. Who made sure they were fed. Who made sure clothes were washed and ironed. Who, three years ago, was so guilt-ridden that she ran her car off the road, committing suicide.

Back when her mother was a student at Marshall College, Charlene had spotted John Maben, who worked at the Marshall College Library, in his living room at the same time Maben was accused of murdering a college student. Charlene had been sneaking back on campus after hours at the time. She was having an affair with a married man, and, even after Maben was tried and sentenced to life in prison, Charlene kept quiet to keep her reputation intact and to graduate from Marshall College. The day Maben died in prison was the day Charlene drove her car off Patterson Bridge into Moore Creek, a forty-foot drop.

Ellen looks at the picture of her mother's sister, Zia, the person she most admires in the whole world. Zia is a broadcast journalist, and Ellen has followed her career from Zia's earlier days with CBS to the time she spent in Cuba as a reporter. CBS sent Zia to Cuba in 1958 to interview Batista. While working in Cuba, Zia met and fell in love with David Foca, a local sugar cane plantation owner. David had been married previously, and he and his wife had two children, Carlota and Julio. David's wife died of cancer years ago.

Zia married David, settling into a new life in Havana. She easily adopted the role of mother to David's children. Zia was standing on the street in Havana in January 1959 when Castro took over Cuba and rolled into the city standing on top of the rolling tank. Along with other citizens, Zia threw red carnations in front of Castro's tank, believing he would bring democracy to Cuba.

Cubans soon discovered Castro was aligned with the Soviet Union, and he would be bringing communism, not democracy, to Cuba. Castro confiscated personal property. He televised live executions and sent some children to the Soviet Union. Thankfully, David and Zia were able to get David's son, Julio, out of Cuba through the Pedro Pan Movement in which thousands of children were flown unaccompanied from Havana to Miami. Julio now attends Marion Military Institute located near Marshall, not far from Ellen's beloved Callander in Alabama.

Castro pulled sugar cane workers from the fields and armed them. The workers were his militia, and he used the militia to terrorize the citizens of Cuba. Zia was running from these militiamen when she stumbled into a friend's restaurant for help and found herself in the middle of a conspiracy to kill Castro.

The militia imprisoned Zia along with the actual conspirators from the restaurant, in La Cabaña, a military prison where Che Guevarra oversaw the execution of Batista loyalists. Before David was able to get her out of La Cabaña, Zia witnessed these men being killed by a firing squad. It damaged her—to the point that Zia hardly communicated with David. She sat and hummed a song and never spoke.

Ellen, while she was on vacation with Luke and other broadcasting students at Montego Bay, had made the risky trip into Cuba to rescue her Aunt Zia. David had managed to get Zia to a friend's home, located on the eastern tip of Cuba, just across from Montego Bay. He had arranged for a fisherman to bring Ellen to Cuba and then return to Montego with Zia in their small boat.

Since April, Zia has been at Callander, and Ellen has Zia back in her life. She's more like the old Zia now, except for the worry lines. She still hasn't heard from David, and it's been six months. But David will never leave Cuba while his daughter, Carlota, is there, and Zia knows this.

Ellen thought about how her aunt was currently researching background information on Brigade 2506, a documentary she hoped to pitch to CBS. Last year, Eisenhower had instructed the CIA to form the Brigade, comprised of more than one thousand Cuban exiles who had fled their country when Castro took power. Now living in Miami, these exiles were the perfect candidates to plot the overthrow of Castro. The failed attempt had occurred in April of last year. The CIA, operating with a budget of $13 million, planned to recruit and train Brigade members to ensure their success in leading an uprising in Cuba.

The CIA conducted infantry training at two bases in Guatemala, an ideal spot to train the recruits; the country was a friend to the United States and its environment was tropical, like Cuba's. The bases were secret. The CIA's code name, JMTRAX, was applied to the training base on the Pacific coast of Guatemala. JMMADD was code for the base for training pilots.

Ellen wonders how Zia is doing with her research. She is thinking about calling home to talk to her when her roommate, Amelia, whirls into the room.

Amelia

"Roomie, what ya doing?" asks Amelia.

"Missing Zia," says Ellen. "Thinking about calling…"

"Oh, Ellen, don't be so mopey. I just had the most fabulous date with Scott. Don't burst my bubble."

"Scott? Which one is he?"

"He's the physical education major. Met him on the tennis courts and, I swear, he's the one."

"Yeah, yeah. Last week Bill the speech major was the one. And the week before it was Joe, the math major."

Ellen sits cross-legged on her bed. She picks up her physics textbook, signaling to Amelia an abrupt end to this conversation.

Ellen and Amelia met last May at a tea held by their dorm mother, Miss Nancy. At the end of her sophomore year, Ellen was assigned to Caldwell Hall for her upcoming junior year. Ann, the best roommate ever, had transferred to the University of Alabama, meaning Ellen had no roommate for her junior year. That was the purpose of Miss Nancy's Tea—the girls could meet each other and find a suitable roommate for the upcoming school year. Caldwell Hall was the dorm of choice, and Miss Nancy has a reputation. Parents stand in line to have their daughters assigned to Caldwell with Miss Nancy, a fierce defender of the honor of any girl under her wing.

Miss Nancy, easily recognized on campus for her six-foot frame and her swing skirts, always with a creative design on them. Miss Nancy always wore crepe-soled loafers to match. She must have dozens of loafers: red ones, blue ones, turquoise ones, yellow ones. Rumor has it that Miss Nancy served in the Navy during World War II. That might account for her strict nature, but she has a nurturing side as well. The two natures clashed at times.

That day of Miss Nancy's Tea, all the junior girls with names that ended in J or K attended. Miss Nancy, her turquoise loafers matching the turquoise daisies on her skirt, greeted them in the lobby.

"Girls, girls. How wonderful! You're here! Please follow me to my suite. We'll have tea, and you can get to know each other."

Ellen looked around the lobby. About fifteen girls are lined up to follow Miss Nancy. The last to fall in line, Ellen noticed a curly-haired girl who looked like a Jackson Pollock painting—colors thrown together—rushing through the dorm door. Was that cigarette smoke Ellen smelled? Definitely. The girl had been smoking. The latecomer looked Ellen in the eye, smiled, and popped a mint in her mouth. Ellen smiled back as the girl shrugged her shoulders. "I'm always late," she said. "It's a fault of mine. My name's Amelia. What's yours?"

"I'm Ellen. Nice to meet you." Ellen liked her.

The girls followed Miss Nancy to her suite of rooms. Miss Nancy had gathered an odd assortment of chairs and placed them in a circle in the middle of the room. As the girls found a seat, Miss Nancy placed a tea tray filled with sugar, cream, lemons—all the things that go with tea time—on a large ottoman in the center of the circle. She then passed out cups filled with hot tea.

Ellen watched in amazement as the girl to her left held the cup in the air and read the label on the bottom. Wrinkling her nose and speaking to no one in particular, the girl said, "These are cheap. Not Grandville, but Potter china." She placed the cup on a table next to her as though it were infectious.

Passing cucumber sandwiches around the circle, Miss Nancy ignored the remark. "I'm thrilled you're here, girls. You'll each have a chance to chat with the other girls and, before you leave, you may fill out the roommate request form. Hopefully, you'll meet someone this very day you'd like to room with."

Well, I sure won't be requesting Miss Grandville!

Miss Nancy stopped in front of Ellen. "Ellen, I'd like you to meet Helen. She's from Alabama, too." Miss Nancy is referring to Miss Grandville girl.

"Where are you from, Ellen? I'm from Mountain Brook," said Helen.

Before answering, Ellen thinks, *Of course, you are.* Mountain Brook, near Birmingham, is one of the most affluent places in Alabama.

"I live near Marshall, Alabama."

"Near Marshall? Not in Marshall?" asks Helen.

"No, I live on my grandfather's plantation."

"Oh, a farm girl. I see." Helen inspected Ellen from head to toe, then turned back to her cucumber sandwiches.

Before Miss Nancy introduced Ellen to another girl, Amelia, the Jackson Pollock girl, chimed in. "After growing up in Coral Gables, I think living on a plantation would be fascinating!"

"I don't know about fascinating, but I love it," Ellen said. "It's the people that make it special. My grandfather, David Henry Callander, owns the plantation, and we have a home on the property along with eleven sharecropper families."

Helen overheard this and said, "Well, farm girl. Do you milk the cows and feed the pigs?"

Ignoring her comment, Ellen got up and walked around the group to meet the other girls. There was a girl named Sue who looked quite athletic, a girl named Mary who is a music major, and a girl named Nancy from Mobile. After meeting the rest of the girls, Ellen sat down again between Helen and Amelia.

Miss Nancy came by, handing a roommate form to each girl. Helen said to Miss Nancy, "I've met the other girls, and I'm willing to room with the farm girl. One must be charitable throughout life."

"That won't be possible, Helen. Ellen and I are rooming together next year." Amelia saved her.

Miss Nancy, her lips pursed in amusement at this exchange, says, "Wonderful, girls! Turn in your forms when you finish them."

Taking the form from Miss Nancy, Ellen glanced at Amelia and mouths, "Thank you."

Ellen looks up at Amelia, flopped across the bed. "Hey, Amelia? Guess what? We have a new anchor in broadcasting, Sandra Rowen. And I think Luke likes her."

"What does she look like?" asks Amelia.

"Gorgeous," replies Ellen.

"What do you mean, Luke likes her? Don't tell me you're jealous."

"I guess not. But you should have seen the way she looked at Luke like he's the best dish on the smorgasbord."

"Ellen, you are not that insecure. Stop worrying about this girl. Luke loves you."

"We have talked about marriage."

"See, you're just silly."

Turning back to her physics book, Ellen says, "Thanks, Amelia. I guess I'm overreacting."

Ellen looks down at her textbook, prepared to read about Newton's laws of motion, but her mind is still on Luke and Sandra. Ellen is not an insecure girl, and she has never worried about her looks too much. People tell her she's attractive, but she's not the Jennifer Jones type. Does Ellen care about looking like a sultry movie star? She does not.

A Call from Home

In the distance, Ellen hears the telephone ring, followed by, "Ellen, the call's for you." Ellen walks down the hall to the telephone booth. She sits down on the worn wooden seat, and picks up the receiver.

"Ellen here."

"Ellen, it's your dad. How are you?"

"Swell, Dad. I did my first stand-upper today. Imagine that! The story is about President Kennedy and fallout shelters. I was so nervous. So afraid I'd forget my lines. I probably psyched myself out, because at one point in the story my mind went blank. The cameraman assured me it was fine. He thought it seemed like a natural pause. I'm not so sure."

"I'm sure you were magnificent. I know you. You're a perfectionist. What did Dr. Shelby say?"

"He was encouraging, but we won't know for sure until the film is developed. How are things at Callander?"

"I have two really important things to tell you. First, Amanda and I will be flying to Miami to visit you at the end of the month. It's been too long since we've seen you."

"Oh, Dad. You've made my day. I can hardly wait to see you."

Ellen's father Will had married Amanda two years after Ellen's mother committed suicide. Amanda, accustomed to dining with sterling, crystal, and china in the dining room had worked to adjust to the Jones family, accustomed to eating off everyday china in the kitchen. Ellen has a good relationship with Amanda, who once aspired to be a broadcast journalist herself.

"Now, for the next piece of news," says Will. "Hold on. It's major."

Ellen holds her breath.

"Zia has heard from David," says Will.

"When? Is he all right? Did he call?"

"No, Zia received a letter. David was in La Cabaña. It seems that Castro imprisoned him this past June after Zia left Cuba. He was only recently released. That's four months in that hell hole. In his letter David told Zia that he's torn. He wants to be with Zia, but he won't leave Carlota."

"Is Carlota still with the Literacy Campaign?"

"David doesn't know where she is exactly, just that she's in some remote area living with various farming families. And yes, she's working with the Literacy Campaign."

With Castro's blessing, Che Guevara had initiated the Cuban Literacy Campaign to address the staggeringly low literacy rate in Cuba. In January 1961, Che recruited adults and children to educate their fellow citizens, mostly in rural areas. Living with families in remote sections of Cuba, the volunteers often work in the fields alongside the family during the day and teach family members to read at night.

When the last illiterate member of a family passes the literacy tests, the family is encouraged to hang a red flag above the doorway of their house to indicate all members of the household can read on a first-grade level. When the last house in a town raises the flag, then the town itself can hoist a larger flag. The town is free of illiteracy.

Ellen had always admired Carlota's dedication to the cause, even if she had not understood her.

"I don't understand, Dad. What makes an upper-class girl work in the fields with the people? She always seemed such a snooty girl to me. I can't visualize her living in a hut and working in the fields."

"I would guess she still thinks Castro is the savior of Cuba. Everyone did when Castro first came to power. Carlota is ignoring all the terrible things that have happened under Castro. She's a young girl with stars in her eyes."

"Maybe, but it's hard for me to understand Carlota. But back to David. What are his immediate plans?"

"Now that he's back in favor with Castro, he's pretty busy overseeing various sugar cane operations. I assume he'll try to find Carlota. That will be hard to do with over two hundred thousand volunteers teaching across Cuba. Say a prayer for David."

"I will, Dad. And thank you for coming to see me soon. I miss you, Amanda, and all the others at Callander."

"Miss you, too. But see you at the end of the month."

Ellen walks slowly back to her dorm room, thinking of David and Carlota and Zia. *Zia*! How relieved she has to be.

Jo Jo

Jo Jo is a sharecropper's son—one of eleven sharecroppers who work on Callander plantation. Ellen's grandfather, David Henry Callander, owns the sprawling farm of 1,200 acres. This plantation land is as essential to Ellen as Tara was to Scarlett. Ellen has lived her entire life in a four-bedroom brick home on the plantation land, but it's the Callander plantation house that she loves most. The house has enormous rooms that smell of fresh flowers in season and the latest baked apple pie to come out of the oven in the huge kitchen.

Callander is a working plantation with a grist mill, a commissary, a syrup mill, a sawmill, a blacksmith shop, and a cotton gin. The coffee-brown soil produces cotton, sugar cane, and any vegetables the sharecroppers grow on their five-acre plots of land. David Henry Callander shelters his people. He provides them with meat, medical care, and, above all else, respect. The sharecroppers are a mix of colored and white families. There is no difference between the two on Callander land, and David Henry protects them from the racial sickness swirling through the country.

Jo Jo and Ellen attended twelve years of school in nearby Marshall, Alabama. Their senior year, they were tapped into the National Honor

Society together. They attended prom together that year, and, standing in the middle of Callander plantation land, Jo Jo had kissed Ellen.

Jo Jo has the build of a star quarterback, which he was, and the powerful aura of a born leader—someone destined for greatness. But then he smiles, his dimple shows, and Ellen knows he's still a Callander man. Seeing him walk the fields in her imagination, it's clear how much he still loves the Callander land.

Jo Jo was a force in Ellen's life during her high school years. She still thinks of him as a vital part of her life, but he is the boy back home. Jo Jo is in the Air Force now, stationed in Tripoli, Libya. Ellen's away at college, and it's all exciting. Luke is one of the most exciting parts of her college life. She's moved on.

On the way back from class, Ellen stops by the old brick campus post office to check her mailbox and is thrilled to see a letter from Jo Jo. Sitting on a bench beneath the moss-draped trees, Ellen reads the letter.

Dear Ellen,

I'm imagining the way you look reading this letter. I sure miss you.

Boy, is Tripoli different from Callander. No lush green trees and plowed fields. Just palm trees and sand. After all, we are on the edge of the Sahara Desert. The great thing, though—Wheelus Air Base is right on the Mediterranean, and the Mediterranean has more shades of blue than can you can imagine.

Bad thing about Tripoli is the scorpions. They're everywhere, and I shake my shoes out every morning before I put them on because Bill found a scorpion in one of his boots. I've been scared ever since.

My duties in the Air Police are okay but not as exciting as my roommate, Bill's. Bill is in AFRS-TV. That stands for Armed Forces Radio and Television. You two would probably hit it off, because he's an anchor for the six o'clock news.

Our television on base consists of reruns of shows like I Love Lucy, Bonanza, Perry Mason, and The Steve Allen Show. We have three live newscasts a day, mostly news that's come into the station from United Press International. Funny thing! There are no commercials. As much as I complained about them in the States, I miss them.

Bill has a radio show called Record Orbit that's popular. He plays all the latest Rock hits and gets postcards from all around the Mediterranean. So glad we have this show. I can keep up with the latest hits and not feel so out of touch.

I knew you'd want me to check out the TV station, so I went over there. It's not very large. I hear it's the only television station in the country of Libya. Amazing! I met the receptionist at the station, an Italian girl named Ilenia. She's gonna take Bill and me on a tour of downtown Tripoli.

They've asked me to play football here. Base personnel have different teams that play against each other. The hospital staff and our Air Police have a team together. I'll quarterback.

Well, that's the news for now.

You're still my girl,

Jo Jo

Thinking of Jo Jo as she walks to her dorm room, Ellen watches a series of pictures floating through her mind—all of Jo Jo. Jo Jo coming to their home to express his sympathy when Ellen's mother died. Jo Jo telling her she's the prettiest in the senior class when she had refused to participate in the Miss Marshall High School Pageant. Jo Jo coming in the back door of Callander plantation with a Christmas gift for her, a poem about leaving Callander.

Ellen enters her room and walks straight to the desk where she keeps her valuables. She sees her books from her Aunt Zia, her family pictures, and a desk plaque with the words "Truth and Honor" engraved on brass. Brushing aside the pictures, Ellen picks up the poem Jo Jo wrote for her.

Leaving Callander

I feel that I can aim high

I never feel that I am just a sharecropper's son

People say that we live in a two-room shack

My parents never say that we are poor

I believe that I am an achiever and will travel far

No one believes that I will see the world beyond Alabama

I've lived so long on Callander land that I know

every inch by smell, taste, touch

I know I could leave if you went with me.

My friends say you'll never look at me

I believe we could live together forever—anywhere.

Reading Jo Jo's poem, Ellen feels the pull of Callander land and its people. She can hear Jo Jo say, with a voice that oozes with images of the South, "You're still my girl."

A Newscast Meeting

Ellen's mind is on Jo Jo and Luke as she walks to the J building the next morning. The two of them are different in so many ways. Jo Jo is a child of Callander, as is Ellen. Luke is from Decatur, Georgia, near Atlanta, and no child of the land. Luke's father owns two local theaters in Decatur, a walk-in theater and a drive-in. Ellen has always envied Luke's childhood; imagine seeing free movies!

It was Luke's mother who had influenced his career choice. She works for the *Atlanta Constitution*, one of the Atlanta newspapers. Growing up, Luke listened to dinner table conversation about whatever story his mother was currently writing. Hard news was a part of his daily life. Ellen understands this.

Walking into the J building, Ellen finds the *Miami News Now* crew assembled in the newsroom waiting for Dr. Shelby. The crew didn't have to wait long. Dr. Shelby strides into the room with his fine, sandy-colored hair flying in all directions, an unlit pipe in his hand. He's wearing his usual tweed sports coat with a vest underneath and his signature bowtie in the school colors of red and black.

"Before we start talking about specific stories in today's newscast, I want to remind you why we're here. *Miami News Now* is a newscast that presents local and national news. But we want to move forward and be more than news readers. We're going to be reporters. We're *Miami News Now,* and we can give our viewers reports of local news they'll never see on the networks. All the more reason to watch us.

I notice a few stories have crept into the newscast that seem more appropriate for a variety show than a newscast. Granted, television is seen as a vehicle for entertainment. I will tell you, I draw a line between shows designed to entertain and newscasts. A heavy line. Our job is to inform. Period. You must produce hard news and feature stories that inform your audience. Unbiased stories. Objective stories presenting both sides of an issue where controversy is involved. Be great! Get all the available facts before you report and be succinct. If our viewers want a variety show, they can tune in to Milton Berle."

Looking around the room at each student, Dr. Shelby continues, "Hopefully, that's enough said about that topic. Now, let's talk about today's rundown. Luke, what's your lead story for today?"

"USSR performed nuclear tests at Kapustin Yar and Novaya Zemlya."

"Good. Watch your pronunciation. And Sandra, your story?"

"*Bye Bye Birdie* closed at the Martin Beck Theater in New York after 607 performances. That's my story. Luke said he'd help me with it." Sandra looks at Ellen, eager to provoke a reaction.

Dr. Shelby takes his lighter out of his pocket and lights his pipe. He only does this when he's stressed. When that lighter comes out of his pocket, watch out. "Sandra, we just had a conversation about airing hard news stories, not entertainment stories. Before you work with Luke, check what's happening locally—like the mayoral run-off. That's important."

Turning to Ellen, Dr. Shelby says, "Ellen, I have an assignment for you. You're going to produce a follow-up to your story on fallout shelters. After the speech from President Kennedy covered in your story, Congress voted for $169 million to locate and stock fallout shelters in public and private buildings. Do you know what a voiceover story is?"

"No, sir. I don't."

"At least you're honest. The story that you recorded earlier about fallout shelters is a reader, because we see and hear you during the entire story. A voiceover story involves the viewer seeing footage that complements the story. The viewer does not see the reporter."

"And we have footage of bomb shelters and fallout shelters?"

"Yes, we do. I've checked this week's reel and noticed quite a bit of footage that complements this story."

The reel Dr. Shelby is referring to comes from United Press Movietone. The Fox Movietone company that produces the newsreels seen in movie theaters had joined forces with United Press to provide footage to television stations. Men called stringers were stationed all over the world, shooting footage of events and then sending the film back to United Press Movietone.

"So, how do we produce this voiceover?"

"Follow me, and I'll show you."

As Ellen stands up to follow Dr. Shelby, she notices Sandra bending over Luke. Her hand resting on his shoulder, her dark hair falling over his face. Ellen's eyes narrow, and she quickly looks away. She doesn't want Dr. Shelby to notice her reaction. *When did she become so insecure?*

Ellen follows Dr. Shelby into an adjacent room, which houses a piece of equipment that dominates the room—a flatbed editor. Moving to the editor, Dr. Shelby removes a 16mm reel of film from its canister and threads the film through the editor's rollers. As Dr. Shelby plays the film, Ellen sees visuals of President Kennedy speaking from the Oval Office, Congress in session, bomb shelters, public buildings labeled with signs that indicate they are designated as fallout shelters, and workers moving boxes of staples into these buildings.

"Ellen, I've written a story. I'll show you how to use the editor. I want you to match footage from the reel to this story:

Congress voted today to earmark $169 million to locate, mark, and stock fallout shelters in public and private buildings. The vote occurred following a speech from the Oval Office in which President Kennedy encouraged citizens to build bomb shelters so that they will be protected from atomic fallout if there is a nuclear exchange with the Soviet Union. President Kennedy assured the citizens that the nation would do its part by marking public buildings as fallout shelters. The Army Corps of Engineers, along with architects and engineers trained by the Corps, will canvass the United States to determine which buildings are suitable to be fallout shelters.

After showing Ellen the basic use of the editor, Dr. Shelby stands back and watches her. Ellen fumbles with the equipment at first, but gradually becomes more comfortable. Dr. Shelby observes her with interest as Ellen chooses a long shot of Congress in action, followed by a medium shot of the President behind his desk in the Oval Office.

Aware that Dr. Shelby is behind her, Ellen turns and says, "I'm in love with editing, Dr. Shelby."

"Well, it seems you do have a knack for it."

"I love this process! Any time you want a voiceover, I'm the one to edit it for you."

As Ellen turns back to the flatbed, she is surprised to hear Dr. Shelby say, "Ellen, you are one of my best students. Sometimes I think you're born to this. Don't let students without your capabilities make you unsure of yourself. Be strong."

Putting his unlit pipe in his mouth, Dr. Shelby walks out of the editing room, leaving a stunned, though somehow comforted, Ellen behind.

There's more to learn about hard news stories and editing in Ellen's Notebook.

Adventures with Amelia

Ellen and her roommate, Amelia, are having dinner in the Tea Room, the large campus dining area lined with red plastic booths and a jukebox at the front center of the room. The Tea Room is *the* place to hang out on campus. You can get a bite to eat and then buy supplies at the attached bookstore. Over the chatter of students in the other booths and "Blue Moon" by the Marcels playing in the background, Ellen and Amelia catch up.

"I met your mother, Amelia," says Ellen.

"Oh, no. Where?"

"When I stopped by the dorm after my first class, Miss Nancy grabbed me and warned me that your mother was in our dorm room."

Amelia groans.

"I tell you, even though Miss Nancy warned me, I was shocked to walk in our room and find this stylish lady with a Jackie Kennedy hairdo hanging curtains. She was accomplishing this by standing on my desk chair."

"Curtains?"

"Oh, yes. This gray fabric covered with wobbly looking rectangles filled with lime and reddish-orange with squiggly lines. Not my choice."

"Don't worry. We'll take them down. My mother has too much time on her hands! Dad's in law, so he's busy all the time. Mother can only decorate or play bridge just so much before she turns her focus to me."

"She was friendly. Wanted to know all about my family and Callander and the broadcasting department. I think she was glad to have someone to talk to."

"She's okay. As long as I'm on campus, and she's in Coral Gables."

"Smothers you, does she?"

"You could say that."

"Oh, another thing. Your mother left us some deviled eggs on one of those plates that have the little semi-circle indentions to put the eggs in."

"Oh, Lawd. Get used to it. Mother thinks she's a deviled-egg connoisseur. Enough about my mother. Tell me about that handsome man of yours."

"He's great. Working on a story all the time. The man lives and breathes broadcasting."

"And the new anchor?"

"Oh, everyone in the department thinks she's got loads of talent. She is good on camera, very professional. Still, she gives me the creeps. A little too femme fatale for my taste."

"Aw, to heck with the broad. If you're worried about Luke, don't."

"Um, thanks for that vote of confidence. I think."

Amelia looks down at the watch on her slim wrist. "Oh, my gosh! Ellen! Look at the time! We've got to run. They close the dorm doors at nine."

Looking around the Tea Room, Ellen sees that they're alone. Grabbing books and purses, they dash out the door. Caldwell Hall is right across the street from the Tea Room. Rushing to the side door, Ellen pulls. It's locked.

"What do we do?" asks Amelia. They're gonna throw us out of school. My mother will hold this over my head for the rest of my life."

"Quiet, Amelia. Let me think."

Looking around, Ellen spots the cylindrical fire escape—an orange, rusted tube standing on end. The fire escape is an object of much amusement to the girls of Caldwell who slide down the twisting, scooped slide that runs from top to bottom inside the fire escape.

"We're gonna climb up that slide, Amelia."

"Are you crazy? We can't do that."

"Sure, we can. Follow me."

Ellen opens the door and crawls inside. Bracing her arms and legs on each side of the cylinder, she starts walking up the slide.

"This is how you do it, Amelia. Follow me up."

"It's slicker than snot," says Amelia.

Ellen doesn't answer. She's concentrating on moving up the cylindrical passage, one careful inch at a time. They're over halfway up when a shout echoes up the fire escape.

"Hey, you. Come out of there right this minute."

"It's the campus police," Amelia whispers from behind her.

Ellen can visualize losing her grip and sliding with Amelia down and out the escape and landing at the officer's feet. Ellen makes a quick decision.

"Follow me, Amelia. We're going up."

Ellen, with Amelia right behind, moves up the slick, curving slide to reach the landing that extends to the second floor.

"Lord, let that door be open," prays Ellen.

Crawling on hands and knees, Ellen reaches the door into the dorm and tugs. It opens. Thank the Lord, it opens. Crawling like giant ants, Ellen and Amelia bump into each other as they scramble into the hall.

Ellen looks over at Amelia, who is floundering on the floor. "Hey, Amelia. I don't think you're kicked out of Columbus U tonight. Now, let's get to the dorm room before we're spotted."

Walking into the familiar room filled with her pictures and books, Ellen is grateful to be back in their dorm room. She's even thankful for those awful drapes hanging in the windows.

The Merrick House Robbery

Not forgetting his promise that the news crew will be reporters as well as readers of the news, Dr. Shelby has assigned Ellen to cover a story about a theft at the Merrick House in nearby Coral Gables.

The Merrick House was originally home to the Reverend Solomon G. Merrick and his wife, Althea, along with their six children. The eldest son, George Merrick, a man of vision, dreamed of building a city with Mediterranean architecture, wide boulevards, and lush landscaping. The town he had envisioned and successfully developed is known today as Coral Gables.

The Merrick House is built of coral rock, mined from a local quarry. When it was finished in 1910, the house itself was named Coral Gables. The family fell on hard times, and in 1935 the house was turned into a boarding house. When Solomon and Althea died, they left the house to their children, who in term gifted the house to their daughter Ethel. The house had remained a boarding house until earlier this year when Ethel died.

Riding the bus to the police station in Coral Gables, Ellen notices the international flavor of this beautiful Miami suburb, with its green spaces, plazas, and spewing fountains. Ellen pulls the rope to indicate to the bus driver that she wants to get off on Salzedo Street, where the Coral Gables Police and Fire Department building is located. The building dominates the block. Made of coral stone, it has the same Mediterranean flair as the rest of Coral Gables.

Walking down the portion of the building on Salzedo Street, Ellen passes three bays for fire trucks. Above the bays are two carved heads of helmeted firemen looking down on passersby. Ellen turns the corner and continues down Aragon Avenue to the police and fire department door. Walking in, she sees a long, wooden desk that extends across the width of the room and serves as the reception area for both the police and fire departments. The extended desk prevents visitors from straying into parts of either department.

An older man and a much younger man are both seated behind the desk. A nameplate identifies the older man as Police Desk Sergeant Baker. Making eye contact and smiling, Ellen walks up to Sergeant Baker, her press pass out for him to see. "Good morning. I'm Ellen Jones from *Miami News Now*, and I'd like to talk to the detective in charge of the Merrick House robbery."

"Well, I think we can accommodate you, young lady. That would be Detective Wofford you want. Just let me ring and see if he's in."

Ellen's first visit to a police department is a little off-putting, even though she doesn't have a criminal bone in her body. She tries to imagine what it would be like for those who walk on the other side of the law to visit the station.

"Ahem." The sergeant clears his throat. "This is your lucky day. Detective Wofford will be right out."

Sergeant Baker busies himself with a stack of papers before looking up at Ellen again. "I don't think I've seen you here before. First time in a police station?"

"Yes. Does it show? Do I look nervous?"

"Just a touch, my dear. Nothing to worry about, though. You're on the right side of the law." He smiles.

Coming out of a hall to the right of the desk is a compact man with greying hair, parted and combed to the right. He has a matching bushy mustache that curves over his upper lip in places. He's wearing a thin, short-sleeved cotton shirt with a sleeveless white T-shirt visible underneath. Ellen's eye goes to the pocket protector filled with pens of varied colors, then her gaze travels upward to his face—its worn features imbued with the hint of kindness.

"Miss Jones, may I present Detective David Wofford. Miss Jones wants to interview you about the Merrick House robbery, detective."

Ellen shows her press pass to the detective before she speaks. Taking the pass, Detective Wofford says, "I follow your news and am usually impressed with the job you folks do. I've met Dr. Shelby several times. He strikes me as a man determined to do an excellent job of informing the public."

Ellen smiles at Detective Wofford, "You have certainly made a correct assessment of our Dr. Shelby," she says. Immediately professional in her demeanor, Ellen asks, "May I interview you about the Merrick House robbery?"

"Of course. Follow me. We'll go to a conference room in the extension part of the building." Lifting a panel at the end of the reception desk, Detective Wofford waits for Ellen to pass through before lowering the board. Ellen follows the detective down the same hall from which he had emerged.

They pass into a small, sterile room with a table positioned in the center of the room. There is a man who appears to be in his seventies emptying the trash in the room. His skin is the color of the caramel icing on the cakes Ellen's Aunt Essie bakes for the family. A stubble of gray hair covers his head and upper lip. Ellen's first impression is that he is a man of elegance. Even with his frayed shirt, often called a guayabera, and the trash can in his hand, Ellen thinks of the word elegance when she sees this man.

"Ellen, meet Mr. Chenard. He tidies up after the very sloppy people in this department."

Mr. Chenard bows at the waist, then straightens. "A pleasure to meet you, my lady."

"I only have a short time to give Ellen an interview, so I hope you'll excuse us, Mr. Chenard."

"Of course, sir. I have finished with this room." Mr. Chenard walks out and softly closes the door behind him.

"Have a seat, Ellen. I have about twenty minutes before I have to be in a meeting. Until then, I'm at your disposal."

Ellen begins, confidently. "I've done my research and know that the house was home to the family of the founder of Coral Gables, George Merrick. I believe the house was deeded to Mr. Merrick's sister, Ethel, who turned the home into a boarding house. Is that right, Detective Wofford?"

"Yes, you're correct. Ethel Merrick died this year, and the house is standing empty."

"And the theft?"

"Well, we don't know the who or the why, but we do know the what, where, and when."

Ellen smiles at the detective's reference to the rules of journalism.

"The theft in question involved breaking in a back door and the removal of two oil paintings hanging in the downstairs hall."

"Can you describe the paintings?"

"Both paintings were done by Althea Merrick, an art teacher who loved to paint the flowers at Merrick House."

"And the when?" asks Ellen.

"We believe it was the night of October 11. The theft was discovered by a family member who came by to check on things on October 12."

"Anything unusual about this case?"

"Yes, the house is filled with paintings, silverware, and objets d'art. Only the two paintings were taken. Seems mysterious to me."

"Any evidence at all?"

"I'll only share that off the record. Can I trust you?"

Solemnly, Ellen nods her head downward and looks up to meet Detective Wofford's eyes.

"It had been raining the night of October 11. Muddy footprints led up the back steps, across the porch, and into the hall."

"And they were made by a man's shoe?"

"No. The footprints were the imprint of a lady's high heels."

"Oh my!" Ellen sits very still. Finally, looking at Detective Wofford, Ellen confesses. "I am embarrassed. I should never assume gender or race. Dr. Shelby would be ashamed of me."

"Well, he'll never know, so stop beating yourself up. It's between us." Detective Wofford smiles at Ellen and she's reminded of her first impression of his worn face with a hint of kindness.

"Thank you, Detective Wofford. For everything. May I come back to talk to you when you catch the thief?"

"You're very optimistic, young lady. Of course you may come back. Can I trust you to see yourself out? I've got to run to my meeting."

"Yes. I don't want to delay you."

Exiting the room after the detective, she walks down the hall toward the building's exit. On the way, Ellen passes Mr. Chenard and catches a faint whiff of cigar, smoked perhaps before he came to work that day. Again, there's the impression of elegance.

There's sure to be a story there.

Jo Jo Goes Downtown

Dear Ellen,

I repeat: I'm imagining the way you look reading this letter. I sure miss you!

I'm gonna try to paint a picture of this land that's so different from Callander. I'll start with downtown Tripoli and its two cities, the old city and the new city. My guidebook says the Phoenicians established the old city called Medina in the seventh century BC. Later, it was part of the Roman Empire. The Medina I'm touring was built on top of the Roman city, and it has two outstanding features. One is The Arch of Marcus Aurelius with its crumbling top. You walk by it entering the northeastern entrance to the market. It reminds me of that famous arch in Paris. It's covered with mythological creatures and was built to celebrate some victory.

The other site is the market. Wow! It's something! Imagine narrow, stone-bordered paths that twist and turn and are lined by one market stall after another. It will blow your wig to try to take in all the different sights, noises, and smells here. Several stalls have spices contained in large, floppy bags—spices like cinnamon bark, rosemary, thyme, and sage. The smells all blend to make a strange scent that's hard to describe.

There are stalls of brass workers, hammering out their designs on the brass trays seen everywhere here. I'll sure try to bring one of these trays home to you. Some of 'em are so large that they're used as coffee tables.

Boy, you would love the stalls of silk dresses and soft, lacy veils. And I'll try to get a Shahi set for you. Shahi is the local tea. It's boiled on low heat and poured from a steel mug to a teapot and from the teapot, held high, back to the mug. This pouring process makes a white, smooth foam that the Arabs like on top of their tea.

As impressive as the Medina is, I will never go there by myself. No airmen go to the old city in uniform because it's not safe there. The locals do not love us.

Ellen, I mentioned Ilenia in my first letter. She works at the base radio and television station, and she's Italian. There's a large group of Italians living here. Came here in the 1930s. Anyway, Ilenia gave us a tour of the new city.

The three of us rode into town in Bill's old 1949 Chevy. The road between Wheelus Air Force Base and Tripoli is one of the few paved highways in the country. It follows the bay into the city.

Driving in the city is insane! It's a good thing Ilenia is used to driving here and knows her way around. The weirdest thing: there are no traffic lights! The first one to get to an intersection and honk their horn has the right of way. It's pretty wild!

We passed by the Uaddan Hotel and Casino. Bill says we'll be spending a lot of time at the Uaddan's nightclub. I'll admit the hotel is impressive with its arches and tall tower overlooking the bay. It's a hangout for airmen on weekends.

Parking facing the bay, we get out of the Chevy and hear a loud, haunting sound coming from what Ilenia says is a minaret. It's a tall, round tower attached to the closest mosque. Ilenia translates what we're hearing:

God is Great, God is Great, God is Great, God is Great
I bear witness that there is no God except the One God.
I bear witness that there is no God except the One God.
I bear witness that Muhammad is the messenger of God.
I bear witness that Muhammad is the messenger of God.
Hurry to prayer. Hurry to prayer.
Hurry to success. Hurry to success.
God is Great. God is Great.
There is no god except the One God.

What strikes me is, except for the Muhammad part, we Methodist believe this. We believe God is great, and there is no God except the one God. Ilenia says the call to prayer or the adhan is performed five times a day to call Muslims to prayer in the mosque. By the way, Islam is the religion, and Muslim is the person. Didn't know that.

Rather than trying to explain what the new city looks like, I'm sending some pictures. You'll get a much better idea of how very different this land is.

Write soon.

You're still my girl,

Jo Jo

Ellen folds the letter and places it back in the envelope. Opening the bottom desk drawer, she puts Jo Jo's letter inside it. Ellen will read it many times. She will add the pictures to her notebook, which is a mixture of notes on broadcast journalism, Zia's photos of Cuba, and now Jo Jo's photos of Tripoli.

See photographs of the Arch of Marcus Aurelius, a minaret, the market, and more in Ellen's Notebook at the end of the book.

Ellen and Luke

"Twist and Shout" by the Isley Brothers blares from large speakers set up on the patio behind the Tea House. Ellen and Luke are in the middle of the crowd of college students gathered on the patio, and they're twisting with abandon. It's fabulous to forget everything and dance. Ellen thinks the world would be a better place if everyone danced more.

The song ends and, as Ellen and Luke move off the patio, Amelia joins them.

"You two look way cool out there twisting," says Amelia.

"Well, I'm glad you think so. You're my next partner," says Luke. Before Amelia can protest, Luke moves Amelia to the dance floor to dance to "The Twist" by Chubby Checker. Ellen watches as these two people she loves have fun with the dance.

As the song ends, Amelia and Luke join Ellen. "You look cool, yourself, Amelia."

"Yeah, yeah," says Amelia. "Before I forget, I need to warn you that Mother stopped by again today. New plants on our desks. And more deviled eggs. This time, they appear to have shrimp on top."

"They'll spoil," says Ellen.

"No, I stuck them in the dorm fridge. You like deviled eggs, Luke?"

"Love 'em," says Luke.

"Well, stop by the dorm. We'll load you up."

"Will do," says Luke. "They're playing our song, Ellen." Luke moves Ellen onto the dance floor, and, as they dance, Ellen rests her head on his shoulder. Luke pulls her closer. She closes her eyes and wonders what it will be like to move through life with this man.

As the song ends, Luke says, "It's a Bowl night. Will you come with me?"

The Bowl is a green space on campus shaped like a bowl. It's where all the couples go to make out. Ellen is not sure about the making out, but something tells her that this time she needs to be in the Bowl with Luke.

"Let me run to my room and get a blanket. Meet you in front of my dorm," says Ellen.

On the blanket at the Bowl, Ellen scoots over and tucks herself under Luke's arm. He bends his head down and kisses the top of her head. They sit that way for a while, just thinking.

"Luke, I love that we both want to be journalists. My Aunt Zia inspired me. I know your mother inspired you. Tell me about it."

"What do you want to know?"

"More about your mother for starters."

"Well, Mother grew up in Decatur. She went to the University of Georgia after high school. She majored in journalism at the Henry W. Grady School of Journalism. You know Mother works for the *Atlanta Constitution*. Considering that Henry W. Grady was once editor of the *Constitution* and built it to be one of the most influential papers in the nation, Mother thinks it quite the honor to work there. She met my father at the University of Georgia. Yes, they're both Bulldogs—and they are pretty obnoxious about it. Mother and Dad met at a frat party and never looked back. They claim it was love at first sight.

My mother adores my father and the rest of us, but we sometimes accuse her of loving hard news more. I wish you could have been at my house for dinner some night. Mother's rules were that my father had to tell us about his day. My brothers and I did the same, then Mother took up the rest of the time with tales about her latest hard news story.

Russia launched Sputnik during my senior year in high school, and the Space Age began. We were all shocked that Russia beat us in putting the first human-made object into space. Mother talked about it for a week. I've only recently realized that Mother taught current events at the dinner table every night. I appreciate the background this gave me in understanding news events today."

"And your father?"

"You know my father owns the local theaters—a walk-in theater and a drive-in."

"I know. I'm so jealous. You got to see all those movies for free."

"But I had to work for it. If I wasn't popping popcorn at the walk-in, I was cooking hot dogs at the drive-in. All of us boys had to work for Dad."

"Tell me about your brothers."

"They're old."

"Luke!"

"Well, they are. My brothers are all married and scattered all over these fifty states. Aaron is the oldest, and he has two boys who adore me, of course. Aaron and Sue live in Birmingham, and Aaron works for the *Birmingham News*."

"And the rest?"

"Ben is in Washington State. He's a writer. Ben has published several nonfiction books on the pioneers that settled that part of the United States. He's married to Ellen—so there'll be two Ellens in the family—and they have a daughter. My youngest brothers are Ed, currently teaching at the University of Texas, and William, who's working on his masters at the University of Georgia."

"I'm impressed with your family, Luke. What an accomplished bunch!"

"And they will be impressed with you. My parents know all about you, you know. They're pushing me to bring you to Decatur. I'd love to show you where I grew up. That said, I think they'll probably come to campus before we can get away to Decatur."

For a moment, Ellen's gut tightens.

It's scary to think about meeting the parents. Luke instantly knows what's running through her mind.

Pulling her closer, he says assuringly, "None of that. I tell you, they'll love you. Mother has always wanted a daughter."

Ellen wraps an arm around Luke's neck, pulling him toward her for a kiss. Looking at her, Luke tucks a strand of hair behind Ellen's right ear.

"Ellen, I know we'll have to wait for sex until we're married. I think I know you that well."

Ellen nods her head slowly. "It doesn't mean I don't want you, Luke. But I think waiting is the right thing to do."

"I'll honor that, Ellen." Luke grimaces. "You don't know how hard it is for me to wait. I love you, and I don't know if you can understand this... I want to feel you under me."

Without breaking eye contact, Ellen lays back on the blanket and waits for Luke to cover her body with his.

Ellen's Family Comes to Miami

Ellen feels the warmth of being surrounded by family. Ellen, Zia, Will, and Amanda are having lunch in an outdoor café in Coral Gables. They sound like a flock of geese, all trying to talk at once with stories bumping into each other and overlapping as they bring Ellen up to date on all the events at Callander.

Zia begins to talk about Thanksgiving. "Just think, Thanksgiving is next month. Julio will be coming to…"

Amanda interrupts her. "Essie is having Thanksgiving dinner at the Mitchell House this year and…"

"You know she will have the old house decorated to the nines," her father says.

"Aunt Zia, tell me about David. That's the news story of the month," Ellen interjects.

"I was on the back porch, where I always write, when Essie brought the letter in from the mailbox. I recognized David's handwriting right away. I started trembling—couldn't even open the letter. Essie had to do it for me. You know he was in La Cabaña?"

"Isn't that the awful prison where you were held, Aunt Zia?"

Zia pales. "Yes. Where I saw men lined against a brick wall and shot by a firing squad. I'll never, ever lose that image. I still see those men shot, staggering and falling to the ground. I still tremble when I think of David in that awful place."

"But he's free of that place. Thank God for that," says Will. Her father is a calming presence for Zia.

"He's supervising sugar cane production, I hear," says Ellen to her aunt. "And Carlota?"

"No news. You know David is trying to find her, but it's difficult. There are over two hundred thousand students out in the countryside teaching the farmers and such."

"Will he come to Callander if he finds her? When he knows she's safe?" asks Ellen.

"I don't think so. David will stay in Cuba."

Ellen stands up and moves behind Zia. She bends down and wraps her arms around her Aunt Zia's shoulders. "But we have *you* at Callander. For that, I am grateful every day."

Zia pats Ellen's arm. "Enough of that," she says. "When do we get to see your young man? I like Luke."

"If you're all up for it, I thought we would go to the beach tonight. We can eat at one of the beach restaurants, build a fire, and sit around and talk."

"I think that sounds like a plan," says Amanda. "What about you, Will?"

"I'm in. I look forward to meeting your Luke again."

Luke had dragged chairs to the beach and had a fire going when Ellen arrived with her father, Amanda, and Zia. After the hellos and hugs, Luke encouraged them to pick their choices from among the restaurants lining the beach.

"Is there a Cuban restaurant?" asks Zia.

"Yes. I'll show you," says Ellen.

"I hope they have medianoche and plantains. I love plantains. I miss the food. All my memories of Cuba aren't bad ones, you know," says Zia.

"We'll stick with hamburgers. You and Ellen go ahead," says Will.

On the walk to the truck, Zia questions Ellen about Luke. "I see he's still as handsome as ever. You as much in love as ever?'

Ellen hesitates. Zia frowns, small lines appearing between her brows. "I repeat, you *are* in love with Luke, aren't you?"

Ellen tucks her arm through Zia's and says, "Oh, of course, I am. But…"

"But?" says Zia.

"I don't want to put my career on the back burner for his. Is that selfish?"

"No, it's not selfish. But what makes you think you'll have to?"

"This is his senior year. He wants to marry after he graduates and take me with him to wherever. Wherever he can find a job in a major market."

"But Ellen. You'll have another year of school."

"Exactly. I don't think I should give that up. I want a job in the industry as well. I can't go where I want to go without a degree."

"And where do you want to go?"

"I'm not sure. I love it all—the investigating, the writing, the editing. Dr. Shelby taught me to edit, and I'm in love with that part of the process. I've yet to direct, but I'll get to do that soon. And I've done a stand-upper. Not so sure about being on-air talent. It's terrifying."

"It's in your blood, child, and I, of all people, know what that's like. I should stay out of it, but I agree that you cannot give up your last year of school."

"It will work out, Aunt Zia. Let's not think about it anymore. We're here to celebrate—celebrate your hearing from David, celebrate all of us being together, and celebrate this Cuban food. I'll try your medianoche and plantains and take enough back for Luke."

"And what is a medianoche?" asks Luke.

"It's pork, ham, and swiss cheese on sweet egg bread. I hope you like it."

"I'm sure I will. And you brought plantains as well? I like plantains. I'll love you forever for feeding me."

"Oh, sure you will, you silver-tongued devil," says Zia with a laugh.

"Ellen tells me you're working on a story to pitch to CBS. Can you talk about it?"

"Of course. It's about Brigade 2506."

"Brigade 2506. That sounds familiar."

"Brigade 2506 is a group of Cuban exiles who fled Cuba and came to Miami. Early last year, when Eisenhower was still President, he authorized the formation of Brigade 2506 and allowed the CIA to train them."

"Was the brigade in the Bay of Pigs invasion?"

"Known in Cuba as the Bahía de Cochinos. Yes, they were. They were the invasion. They surrendered after less than twenty-four hours of fighting. Castro captured most of the Brigade members and imprisoned them in Havana."

"I know the Bay of Pigs was a disaster for the United States. Didn't Kennedy oppose the plan?" asks Luke

"When Kennedy became president, he saw the situation differently than Eisenhower had seen it. Kennedy feared the Soviets might see the invasion as an act of war," says Zia.

"But he went ahead with it."

"The CIA assured Kennedy they could keep their involvement out of it. If the invasion had been successful, an anti-Castro rebellion would have occurred at the same time. I assume President Kennedy weighed the odds and decided to go ahead with the plan."

"What went wrong?"

"The first part of the plan involved taking out Castro's air force. If that had happened, the invasion might have been successful. A group of the exiles took off from Nicaragua in American planes painted to look like Cuban planes."

"And what happened?

"Castro heard of the plan and moved his planes to safety before the strike."

"This is certainly a story worth telling. What will you do for footage? Do you have sources?"

"I'll use archival footage from CBS if they take the story. Yes, I have sources. I'm interviewing a few survivors of the invasion right here in Miami tomorrow. Would you like to come?"

"You're serious. You'll let me come?"

"You have press credentials, don't you?"

"Sure."

"I'll bring you as my assistant!"

"I can't thank you enough. Wow! A chance to hear the story first-hand."

Zia smiles at Luke's enthusiasm. "Don't think I won't put you to work, though."

"Anything you need."

"I'll pick you up at the J building tomorrow around ten o'clock. That will work out nicely as Will and Amanda are visiting the studio there tomorrow morning."

Ellen leaves her father and Amanda and walks around the fire to talk to Zia and Luke.

"What are you two talking about? You're thick as thieves."

"Your Aunt Zia is taking me on an interview tomorrow morning. It has to do with the documentary she's working on," says Luke.

"Well, aren't you the lucky one? I think I'm jealous."

Luke stands up and pulls Ellen to him. "I'll tell you all about it. I promise."

Zia stands and says, "This has been the loveliest evening. I've loved every second of it, but it's past my bedtime. Will and Amanda are probably ready to join me. Ellen, do you mind running us to the hotel?"

"Of course not. Luke, you want to come?"

"No. Think I'll stay on the beach for a while. I'll look forward to tomorrow, Aunt Zia—if I may call you that. And Ellen, don't you leave without kissing me goodnight."

"Well, I'll leave you and let you say goodnight in private," says Zia.

As Zia leaves, Ellen falls into Luke's arms. "Let me stay here just a minute."

Luke wraps his arms tight around her, pressing her body against his. "I love you, Ellen Jones."

Kissing him on the nose, Ellen says, "And I love you, too. Gotta go."

Pulling her back, Luke covered Ellen's mouth with his. She loves the feel of his soft lips on hers and the way his body feels pressed to hers. Slowly backing off, Luke releases Ellen.

"Now you can go. See ya later."

Mr. Chenard

Walking down Salzedo Street on her way to the Coral Gables Police Department, Ellen looks up at the two carved heads of helmeted firemen situated above the firehouse bays. For the first time, she notices the other carvings nearby. They appear to be a family. Ellen turns the corner and heads for the door of the joint police and fire departments.

Walking in, she sees the same police sergeant sitting behind the long desk. "Good morning, Sergeant Baker. I have an appointment with Detective Wofford this morning."

"I know you do, young lady. You'll be in the same conference room. I'll walk you down."

"Thank you, Sergeant Baker."

"You remembered my name. Good for you. Remembering names is important if you're a reporter. Well, here we are. I'll leave you to it."

Ellen grabs Sergeant Baker's hand and shakes it. "Thank you for making me feel welcome, Sergeant." Ellen can tell the Sergeant is pleased with her gesture. As he walks away, Ellen enters the conference room to find Mr. Chenard cleaning the room. Again, she thinks of elegance as she notices the way he is holding the trash can.

"I believe you're Mr. Chenard, am I correct?"

"Yes, I am he," replies Mr. Chenard in a cultured voice.

"I'm pleased to see you again, Mr. Chenard. May I ask, have you worked here long?"

"For two years. Since I arrived from Cuba."

"Cuba! My Aunt Zia was in Cuba until April of this year."

"She was? She is no longer there?"

"No, she's in the United States. It's a long story—a story for another day. But you? How did you come to Miami?" Ellen pauses. "I'm sorry if I'm too forward, Mr. Chenard," she adds quickly. "It's a habit of mine."

"Do not worry, Miss Ellen. I have no compunction in talking about my life. Now, how did I come to Miami? A man who worked for my father owned a six-foot motorboat, and he, too, wanted to leave Cuba to live in the United States, where he had relatives."

"So, that's how you escaped?"

"Yes, but I tell you, we had to work up our courage. Leaving Cuba is a crime. Just talking about it, much less helping someone escape, is a crime. If caught, you could spend up to ten years in prison."

"But you left anyway?"

"I had to leave. To protect my family. That is a story for another day." Mr. Chenard smiles upon repeating Ellen's earlier statement to him. "But Carlos, who worked for my father, just wanted the adventure. He wanted to live in the United States with his relatives."

"You couldn't know this, but I've been to Cuba. I was terrified. Was your departure a hard trip?"

"I see we have many stories to share. Yes, it was difficult. The first twelve miles out, the waters are owned and patrolled by Cuba. We left at three o'clock in the morning, hoping the darkness would help us escape. It did, and we were fine until about five miles off the coast of Key West."

"You were almost captured?"

"No. The boat sprung a leak. Carlos paddled, and I used a bucket to bail water. That boat sunk within sight of the shore. Carlos and I swam for it."

"Luck was with you, Mr. Chenard."

"I assure you, I know that very well."

"What's the rest of the story?"

"The simple version is that a fisherman found us and took us to his family in Key West. We did not know how we would get to Miami. We had little money, and the money we had was pesos, not U.S. dollars."

"How did you get to Miami? That's over fifteen hundred miles from Key West."

"The fisherman knew someone with a truck who agreed to take us. Think about it. That fisherman took us in. We spent the night in his home. He fed us and clothed us. That fisherman holds a special place in my heart to this day. My first introduction to the United States was warm, indeed."

"But how do you sur… ?" Ellen stops talking abruptly, appalled at the question she was about to ask

"How do I survive?"

"Please pardon my rudeness. That's personal. I had no right to ask."

"I will answer you anyway. Your government—that is how I survive for now. They found this job for me and give me a small pension to live on. I am keeping a record of every cent given to me from the government and will pay it back. All of it."

"You're paying it back?"

"Yes, Miss. I have to if I want to hold my head up. I might add that the government is helping me attend classes so that I can teach in the United States."

"Oh! You're a professor."

"Yes. I taught literature at the University of Havana."

"More story to tell?"

"Yes, but another day. Here's Detective Wofford. Nice talking with you, young lady."

"May I talk with you again?" She turns to the detective. "Detective Wofford, would that be all right?"

"And hello to you, Ellen."

"Hello, Detective Wofford. Thank you for seeing me today."

The detective smiles. "As long as you talk to Mr. Chenard on his own time, you're welcome to come to talk with him here at the station."

Ellen smiles back at the detective. His answer reaffirms her assessment of the detective. He's seen so much in his line of work but has retained a kindness. Ellen detects this from the smile topped by the bushy mustache curving over his upper lip, something she had noticed on her first visit to the station.

"Why don't you talk to Mr. Chenard some Friday? He only works in the morning."

"Could I, Mr. Chenard? I can be here by two o'clock on any Friday that you can meet with me."

"What's an old man got to do? Of course, I will meet with you."

"I warn you. I want to ask about your life in Cuba."

"A story for another day, Miss Jones. I look forward to seeing you this Friday?"

"Yes. I'll wait at the desk for you. I'll be there at two."

"Fine, young lady. I will see you at two."

"Ellen, that's nice of you to take time with Mr. Chenard."

"I enjoy it. That's one reason. But don't forget, I'm a reporter. I know your Mr. Chenard has quite a story to tell."

"Still nice of you, even though you have ulterior motives. Mr. Chenard's all alone, you know."

"No, I didn't know."

"Meeting with you will be a highlight of the week for him."

"I'll remember that, Detective Wofford. Pausing, she says, "Now, about the Merrick House robbery."

The detective laughs out loud. "You are the consummate reporter."

Ellen smiles at him. "Did you solve the robbery?"

"Yes, but anything I tell you is off the record."

"So, I can't write and publish a story about what you're going to tell me?"

"Correct. Some journalists think they can report an off-the-record comment as long as they don't reveal the source. I assure you that's not what I mean here. Now, do I have your word?"

More serious than before, Ellen answers, "Yes, sir. You do."

This is the second time Ellen has encountered this situation with the detective, and she recognizes at once the trust the detective has in her.

"I remember George Merrick founded Coral Gables, and that, on October 11, two paintings were stolen from his family home. George's mother, Althea, painted these two paintings as well as others scattered throughout the home. These were the only two things stolen from the home."

"Correct so far. I was surprised myself that nothing else was taken," the detective replies. "The house is filled with expensive items."

"And the muddy footprints—the high heels. Did you find the thief?"

"Yes, but remember we're off the record. A distant cousin of Ethel and George stole the paintings. According to her confession, Althea had played an important role in her young life, and she wanted a remembrance."

"And she'll be sentenced?"

"No. Remember, Ethel is dead, and the estate manager decided the cousin should have the paintings. So, that's the end of that mystery."

"So, the cousin is getting off scot-free?"

"Not totally. To avoid prosecution, the cousin has agreed to inventory the family house."

"And they trust her?"

"I guess they do. Anyway, they closed the case."

"So, no follow-up for *Miami News Now*."

"That's okay. If I'm not mistaken, you've found a much more interesting story right here at the department."

"Mr. Chenard?" Ellen pauses. "Yes, I agree. Did you know he was a professor of literature at the University of Havana?"

Smiling, the detective says, "Did you know that more than half the entire faculty of the University of Havana live in or near Miami today?"

"No. Surely, that's not correct."

"I assure you, it is. May I ask why you're so interested in Mr. Chenard's story?"

"My aunt was in Cuba. She was imprisoned in La Cabaña. After she was released, I worked with her husband to get her out of Cuba. I went into Cuba to get her out."

"And you were successful?"

"Yes, she's at the family home in Alabama right now."

Detective Wofford seems stunned by this news. He doesn't speak for a while. "I knew there was more to you than meets the eye. I see why you'd like to talk to Mr. Chenard."

"Thank you so much for understanding and for letting me talk to him here at the station."

The detective nods at Ellen. "It's my pleasure, Ellen."

Ellen turns and shakes the detective's hand before saying goodbye. She leaves the conference room, grateful to have met the detective and eagerly awaiting her conversation with Mr. Chenard.

NOVEMBER 1961

Hoyt v. Florida

Ellen walks into the broadcasting studio and spots Luke working in a cubicle. She has not seen him since the family night at the beach. She's curious to know about his visit with Aunt Zia to interview participants in the Bay of Pigs.

Luke spots Ellen before she reaches the cubicle. "Cotton, Hi! Want to give me advice on this article?"

"I will, but first I want to know about your visit with Aunt Zia to interview the Brigade 2506 members."

"It was interesting."

"That's all you can say? It was interesting. I'd think just the opportunity to watch Aunt Zia in action would be exhilarating."

"I'll admit. Zia's a real professional."

"So, tell me all about it."

"I don't have anything to say. It was interesting."

"And that's all you're going to say?"

"I don't want to talk about it, Cotton. Would you give me your advice on this story?"

Puzzled, not to mention more than a little hurt by Luke's attitude, Ellen stares at him. Luke bends his head over the story he's working on.

"Well, obviously you aren't going to talk to me about your time with Aunt Zia. So what story are you working on, and how can I help?"

"I thought it might be a good idea to get a female perspective. My story is about the Supreme Court case, *Hoyt v. Florida*. Familiar with it?"

"Something about an all-male jury. Am I right?"

"Right as rain, Cotton. The case took place in the 1950s but was just decided by the U.S. Supreme Court this month. Gwendolyn Hoyt was convicted of murdering her husband over an affair her husband was reportedly having, and she was sentenced to thirty years of hard labor. Mrs. Hoyt claimed that her fundamental rights were violated because only men served on the jury."

"Well, weren't they violated?" asks Ellen. "What if the case were reversed? A jury of all women convicted a man accused of murdering his wife over an affair. People would raise hell."

"It's just not that simple. The state of Florida requires men to register for jury duty, whether they want to serve or not. Women, on the other hand, can register if they want to serve, but the state of Florida does not require women to serve."

"That's ridiculous. Women can serve as well as men."

"I think the idea is to keep women safe in the home—not expose them to all the nasty things that occur in court."

"Baloney. That's archaic!" Ellen says. "What about due process and equal protection under the law? The 14th Amendment and all that."

"That was Gwendolyn Hoyt's point. The Supreme Court disagreed with her."

"Why?"

"Mrs. Hoyt had the right to an impartially selected jury, but she did not have the right to a jury tailored to her case. By the way, not many women were available to be chosen for a jury trial. Most of the women didn't register in the 1950s. After all, women could register if they wanted."

"But Luke, she was not represented by a fair cross-section of the community where she was tried."

"But Ellen, Mrs. Hoyt was tried in Hillsborough County. There are more than ten thousand jurors eligible to serve, but—and here's the kicker—only ten of those were women."

Luke looks at Ellen, a smug look on his face. Ellen hates that smug look, his tight-lipped smile and a look that says *I'm superior to you.* Ellen has to make that look disappear, at least for now, at this moment, before she can respond.

"Well, I tell you Luke, when we marry or *if* we marry, wherever we land, you can count on me registering for jury duty!"

Swirling around, Ellen races across the room, distancing herself from Luke as quickly as she can. Cooling down, Ellen thinks of Aunt Zia, the strongest woman she knows. Would she have registered for jury duty? Of course. And what about Aunt Essie? Yes. Ellen remembers Essie serving on a civil case just last year. Ellen snorts. Women not serving on juries? Not her people.

The Ladies of Libya

Dear Ellen,

Just thinking of you and thinking about what a strong woman you are. That makes me want to tell you about the women in this country. I'll start with the Arab women. I can't describe them in any detail because the ones I've seen cover themselves from head to toe in something called a barracan. It's a white wool garment that covers everything except their right eye and their feet!

On a side note, men wear barracans, too. The barracans on men drape over the head and shoulders and hang near the knee. Some men wear pants that are the strangest things you've ever seen—the crotch hangs down near the knees. Rumor has it that the pants with the low-hanging crotch will catch the baby Muhammed, who will be reborn to a man. Who knows if this is true?

You don't see a lot of Arab women on the streets here. The streets, the cafes, and the shops are the domain of the male. Any Arab women that you do see are covered head to toe, and a kinsman always accompanies them. The woman's domain is in the family compound. Upper-class women are secluded from puberty to menopause in a custom called Purdah. The meaning of the word Purdah is the curtain, which is appropriate for this custom of keeping women hidden from men outside of the traditional family. Arab women practicing Purdah spend much of their time together, sharing sewing, music, and their life stories. A strong bond exists among these women.

Even in the home, women live in curtained-off areas. Only members of the immediate family may interact with the women. When male visitors come to the house, women remain behind the curtain. Any woman who serves the guests must do so wearing a barracan.

I can imagine you reading this, Ellen, and comparing Purdah to your life in the States. You'll be surprised to learn that Purdah is liberating for the Arab women, who are judged by their inner beauty and intellect as opposed to their physical beauty. The woman wearing the barracan is mysterious. I find this life so fascinating. I am learning a lot for a boy raised at Callander!

I hear King Idris' wife, Fatimah el-Sharif, is an exception to most upper-class Arab women. I'll admit she fascinates me. I've done some research. Queen Fatima is younger than the King and, surprisingly enough, wears Western clothes and socializes with American women. She was born in Tripoli to Ahmed Sharif as-Senussi, the former chief of the Senussi order of Sufism. She married King Idris when she was twenty years old. The king is her first cousin. I don't know if marrying cousins is standard practice here or not.

The queen and the king only had one child—a boy, who sadly only lived to be one day old. Although they adopted children, they had no biological children, and this became important as Idris became King twenty years into their marriage. Idris needed an heir.

Fatima encouraged Idris to marry again to obtain an heir, and she even picked out two candidates for the King to marry. Idris married neither. Instead, he married an Egyptian lady, Aliya Effendi. They married in 1955, had no surviving children, and King Idris divorced her in 1958. He was still married to Fatima during his marriage to Aliya.

Fatima attends public events and is good with the people of Libya. She is outgoing and serves as a role model for young Libyan women. No wearing a barracan for Fatima.

Ilenia, who works at the base television station, is different from the majority of Libyan women as well. I guess that's because she's Italian, even though she's lived her entire life in Tripoli. There's quite a large number of Italians in Tripoli, and here's why...

In 1910 the Italians attacked Libya to liberate it from Istanbul. They had ruled Libya until the Allies won World War II and Italy had to give up Libya. Mussolini paid a visit to Tripoli and had a highway built that ran from Tripoli to Benghazi. You know Mussolini was the fascist ruler of Italy, but you probably didn't know this: Mussolini was Hitler's role model. Hitler got his Sieg Heil salute from Mussolini.

Sorry, I'm rambling... Ilenia graduated this year from Lecio High School, the Italian high school in Tripoli. According to her, it's an excellent school. She wants to go to college and major in broadcast journalism. That's why she's working at the station.

Ilenia loves photography. I wish you could see some of her work. My favorite is a close-up of an elderly man who sells spices in the old city. The eyes of this old man and the age rivulets in his face—so much character there.

She has a little of the glamour that you see in Gina Lollobrigida. Some of the guys around the station even call her Gina. I think she likes the nickname. She sure smiles when someone calls her that. Ilenia dresses just like the American girls over here. I think she's a strong woman who knows where she wants to go in her life. You two have that in common.

I got to run.

Hugs to you, sweet girl,

Jo Jo

Ellen folds the letter and returns it to its envelope.

What happened to "You're still my girl?"

See more pictures of Tripoli in Ellen's Notebook at the end of the book.

Mr. Chenard

Ellen has kept her Friday appointment with Mr. Chenard. It's not likely that she would forget. She's been looking forward to unraveling his story. Mr. Chenard is telling Ellen about Cuba as he remembered her before he came to Miami. He always refers to Cuba as feminine.

"I tell you, Ellen, I hardly knew Cuba when I left her. That is how much she changed."

"Can you tell me about it?"

"You have to understand how my life was before Castro. I come from a long line of professors, most of whom taught music or literature at the university level. My father was a literature professor, too. As a family, we lived and breathed the arts. Classical music constantly played in our home on the radio. After Castro, no classical music. Or any music. for that matter. Only propaganda on the radio after Castro."

"What a terrible way to live! I grew up listening to all types of music, from Johnny Cash to Tchaikovsky. I can't imagine living without music."

"And there is so much more. Theatres populated Havana. Our family routine involved going to church in the morning and attending a play in the afternoon, all types of plays. Plays from France, even. After Castro, all the theatres were closed. Not one left open."

"So, no plays on Sunday afternoons, and our Sunday mornings changed as well. Castro brought the sugar cane workers in from the fields and armed them. They were the new militia. The militia lined the walk outside of the church and spat on us as we walked between the two lines after church. That is how radically our life changed, almost overnight.

And, of course, all property was confiscated, just taken by the government. Property that had been in families for generation after generation, all taken. Businesses, too. Nothing owned by the individual anymore. All government-owned. And the executions were televised for all to see. So brutal. Family members were not allowed to bury their loved ones. The government buried the executed ones in mass graves—no family graves to adorn with flowers and shed tears over."

"I'm so sorry you lived through that, Mr. Chenard. So very sorry. You were at the University of Havana?"

"Yes, I taught literature. The educational system changed, as well. The children were taught the alphabet like this—"C is for Castro, and Y is for Yanqui," Yanqui being the enemy: the people of the United States. Castro began closing all the private schools, most of which were operated by the Catholic Church. All schooling involved the children learning Marxism. Parents began sending their children out of Cuba."

"Mr. Chenard, I know about the Pedro Pan Movement. My nephew, Julio, was one of the thousands of children that left Cuba."

Eyebrows scrunched together, Mr. Chenard says, "Really?"

"Yes, sir. Before Castro came to power, my Aunt Zia married David Foca, a sugar cane plantation owner in Cuba. David has two children, Carlota and Julio, and Aunt Zia and David feared for the children. Castro was sending some children to the Soviet Union for training in camps. Carlota quickly became entrenched in the Marxism doctrine. She's very argumentative, and David had little control over her.

Zia and David flew Julio out of Cuba to Miami to save him. He has quite the story to tell. He's in a school near where I grew up. You'd like him, Mr. Chenard. We all adore him. No doubt, he's part of our family."

"No wonder you are interested in my story. You are involved."

"Yes, sir. But about your teaching? You mentioned things changed in education as well."

"Yes. Castro realized that education could play an important role in the revolution, and he changed the courses I could teach at university."

"In what way?"

"I could teach literature, but only if it supported a socialist way of life. The government provided me with a list of literary works I could teach in my classes. In truth, I do not think Castro saw a great need for education at the university level."

"Could you do that, Mr. Chenard? Teach only from a list given to you by Castro?"

"No, Ellen. I could not do it. How could I not expose my students to the great literature of the world?"

"Did you get in trouble?"

"Eventually, I would have. I probably would have been sent to La Cabaña."

"La Cabaña. My Aunt Zia was there."

More scrunched eyebrows. "Ellen, your aunt was in La Cabaña?"

"Yes, she innocently went into a restaurant where Cubans and CIA representatives were plotting to kill Castro. She was caught up with the plotters and taken to La Cabaña. She witnessed executions firsthand, and it scarred her. My uncle got her released and took her to Oriente, where he owned a sugar cane plantation before Castro took it. David Foca is my uncle's name. He has people loyal to him in Oriente, and they looked after Aunt Zia until I could come to get her."

"What? You went to Oriente to get her?"

"I did. It's probably better I don't tell you all of the stories. Tight lips and all."

"I knew you were a special young lady. I have to tell you I admire you very…"

"Now, Mr. Chenard. You know we do what we have to do."

"No, Ellen. Don't make the mistake of thinking everyone is like you, with your courage and intelligence."

Ellen bows her head, touched by Mr. Chenard's comment. After a moment, Ellen looks up. "Mr. Chenard, I love talking to you, and I have a serious question to ask you."

"Well, go ahead, young lady."

"I would like to produce a news story, a feature story, about you and Cuba. About how you love her—that comes through when we talk—and how you had to leave her."

"Who would see this story?"

"It would air on *Miami News Now,* and I'd like to submit the story for a Peabody Award."

"Something to think about, Ellen. My wife and children are still in Cuba. May I let you know?"

"Certainly. I won't be back to see you until after Thanksgiving. Could we talk again then?"

Standing, Mr. Chenard says, "Ellen, I assume you are going home for Thanksgiving?"

Ellen says, "Oh, yes. I am going home to Callander, my grandfather's plantation in Alabama. There will be so much food and so much love. You know, I'd love to take you with me one day. You'd adore the whole bunch."

"Thank you for the thought. You can think of me celebrating with my adopted Cuban family here. We celebrate Thanksgiving with a Cuban flair."

"I'll do just that," Ellen says laughing. "And, until I see you again, take care."

Ellen reaches to shake hands with Mr. Chenard. He takes her hand in his right hand and covers her hand with his left, then squeezes. When Mr. Chenard releases her hand, Ellen turns to pick up her things, hiding the emotion she feels. She is growing so fond of this lovely man.

Ellen looks back over her shoulder as she walks out the door. "Goodbye, Mr. Chenard. See you after Thanksgiving."

Visit Ellen's Notebook at the end of the book to see Mr. Chenard's Cuba.

Hide Your Panties

As Ellen enters Caldwell Hall, Miss Nancy, the dorm mother, is walking through the first-floor lobby, shooing out all the males. True to form, she's wearing her swing skirt adorned with red and blue kittens around the hem. Her crepe-soled loafers are red, the same red as the gamboling kittens. One can set their watch by Miss Nancy: it never fails. At nine o'clock, she's in the main lobby running off the males.

Ellen likes Miss Nancy. She appreciates her fierce protection of the girls and loves to tease her. "Miss Nancy, a senior boy is hiding behind that column."

"Get away with you, Ellen. I know you're teasing me."

Ellen walks up to Miss Nancy and reaches up to hug her. Miss Nancy loves the attention but she is rattled by it. Gathering herself, she warns Ellen. "I want you girls to be vigilant tonight."

"Why is that, Miss Nancy?"

"Rumors are rolling across campus. There's going to be a panty raid at Caldwell tonight."

Ellen swallows to keep the grin off her face.

"Surely not, Miss Nancy. A panty raid?"

"Yes. I'm afraid it's a senior tradition. The senior males pick a dorm and raid it."

"Raid it?"

"I'll spell it out. The boys come into your dorm room, open your dresser drawers, and steal a pair of your panties."

Ellen laughs out loud. She can't help it.

"It's not funny, Ellen. What will your parents say if I allow these boys to steal my girls' panties?"

"I think they'll understand it's a prank and not your fault."

"You don't know some of these parents. Anyway, it's not going to happen. Not in my dorm."

Smiling, Ellen says, "I believe you, Miss Nancy. I know you'll protect us."

Walking down the hall to her room, Ellen laughs again. The whole idea of a panty raid sounds like great fun. Amelia unleashes her story as soon as Ellen enters.

"My mother has done it again. She left these horrid green pillows on our beds. I assume Mother chose them to match the drapes. Yuck!"

"It's okay, Amelia. Don't worry about it. We've more important things to talk about. Have you heard about the panty raid tonight?"

"Why, yes. And I'm ready." Amelia opens her top dresser drawer to reveal bunches of frothy, lacy panties in all colors—pink, blue, purple, yellow, and even orange.

"Amelia, do you actually wear those things? They look downright uncomfortable."

"Trust me, they are. More of Mother's purchases for me. Trying to make me something I'm not. I had stuffed them away but dug them out when I heard about the raid. Want some?"

Ellen pulls out her own underwear drawer and looks at the white cotton panties lining the drawer. She doesn't miss a beat.

"Sure thing. Share with me."

A room off the front porch has its advantages. Around eleven o'clock that night, Ellen and Amelia hear feet coming up the cobblestone sidewalk to the dorm, lots of feet. Shushing sounds. A doorknob turned repeatedly. Then, "The damned door is locked."

"Whatta we gonna…"

"We gotta get…"

"Keep your voices down."

"You guys hang tight. I'm going to see if I can get in through the dining hall."

The dining hall is attached to Caldwell Hall. All the girls are seated here for a family-style meal at night. Some of the best food in Florida is served in the dining hall at Caldwell.

Ellen peaks through the hideous curtains to see maybe forty or fifty boys milling around in front of the dorm. And sure 'nuff there's Luke, right there with the rest of them. Ellen's heart skips a little beat, just looking at him. He is a fine-looking man.

"Hey, I'm going for Betty Todd's panties. Her roommate told me where her room is."

"I'm gonna rip the panties off the first girl I see."

"Hell, I'm not doing that."

Evidently, a door was open in the dining hall area. Ellen and Amelia hear the boys chattering about opening the front door. Then suddenly, an ear-splitting yell. Ellen sees the boys with mouths open, skin taut around the mouth. They roar collectively as they bound up the stairs and spurt into the dorm. They look like conquerors.

Girls' screams mix with the boys' roars.

"We gotta see what's happening, Ellen."

Amelia opens the door to their room. Ellen comes up behind her, peering over the top of Amelia's head. Their hall is quiet. Cautiously, they make their way to the lobby. Unbelievable! Like a scene from the second ring of hell. There are guys swarming like bees—up the staircase, down the halls that branch to the left and right. Girls screaming at the top of their lungs. Other girls throwing their panties at the boys. Miss Nancy has claimed the top of the staircase as her domain, and she's throwing pots at the boys over the railing—pots with dirt and flowering plants inside.

"That woman's crazy."

"She's trying to kill us."

"A pair of panties ain't worth this."

As quickly as the dorm filled with senior boys, it has emptied. Ellen and Amelia go back to their room and close the door. Outside their door, they hear, "Come on, Luke. We have to go. What the hell are you doing?"

The door to Ellen and Amelia's room bursts open and Luke is standing there grinning.

"Come on, Ellen. One pair of panties."

In the blink of an eye, Ellen pulls open her panty drawer and tosses Luke a pair of the lacy panties.

Luke bows. "Thank you, ma'am." Then he's off.

Ellen looks out the front window. There is Luke, running across the lawn in front of Caldwell, twirling Ellen's panties in the air. To the conquerors go the spoils.

Luke and Ellen

The day before Ellen leaves for Thanksgiving, Luke and Ellen are sitting on a bench outside Caldwell Hall. Luke will stay in Miami for the holiday, working for the station he worked for this past summer.

"I hear Dean Walker came around the mens' dorms checking shoes last night."

"News travels fast. He did that."

"Did you get caught?"

"Luke the Legend is too smart to get caught. Dean Walker was checking shoes to see if they were damp, so he could identify the raiders. Ergo, if the owner of damp shoes had been out at night, the owner was in trouble."

"And?"

"I hid my wet tennis shoes under my mattress and put the dry pair in my closet."

"And that worked?"

"Why, yes. Dean Walker said he knew I was involved, but he couldn't prove it."

Ellen blushes. "And the panties?"

"They'll never see the light of day, Cotton. I promise you that."

"Good." Ellen scooches over and places her head on Luke's shoulder.

Luke turns his head and kisses her forehead. "Let's talk about our wedding."

"I liked Dad and Amanda's wedding, on the porch at Callander."

"I remember the baby grand piano on the front porch. Very classy!'

"And I loved that Amanda walked through the double front doors onto the porch to the strands of wedding music. But I don't want to do the exact same thing. Every bride wants her wedding to be original."

"Have you thought about having the wedding at the Methodist church? We could still have the reception at Callander in the ballroom."

"It's an idea. The church is very special to me. I always remember Mother directing the Christmas plays. I was an angel."

"Of course, you were." Luke kisses Ellen on the forehead again and works his way down to her mouth. "Yum! You taste like an angel."

"Seriously, Luke, your idea is not a bad one. I'd feel Mother was there with us."

"You can think about it. We've got time."

Not wanting to discuss when they were getting married on this last night before she left for home, Ellen changes the subject. "Let's talk about the wedding party."

"Your Dad will give you away. Who will be the Maid of Honor?"

"My childhood friend, Liz. What about you? Who will be the best man?"

"My oldest brother, Aaron."

"How about ushers?"

"The rest of my brothers."

"I look forward to meeting them. I guess this will be the first time I'll see all of your family together."

"Probably so. I can't wait for the entire bunch to meet you. I'm proud of you, Ellen."

"Why, thank you, Luke." Ellen doesn't delve into why Luke's proud of her. It's enough right now that he is.

"Oh, and music. We haven't talked about music at our wedding," says Ellen. "Whither Thou Goest" is the song everyone but everyone includes in their wedding. I want something different. The song I want is "When I Fall in Love." That will be the song we dance our first dance to at the reception. Do you remember why I want this song for our first dance?"

"How could I forget? It's the song we danced to at your father's wedding, when you told me you loved me," says Luke.

"Luke, you remembered." Ellen gets misty-eyed as she stands up and pulls Luke toward her, wrapping her arms around his neck.

Ellen leans back in Luke's arms and looks up at him. "Did I ever tell you that we already have furniture?"

"No. I'd remember that."

"This summer I cleaned the attic of the plantation house and found dining chairs, a Duncan Phyfe Chest, and Christmas ornaments—little porcelain men dressed in trousers and coats with long tails and top hats. Adorable!"

"What's a Duncan Phyfe Chest, and will I like it?"

"Duncan Phyfe was a man who lived in the 1800s. He created some of the most sought-after furniture ever. You'll like it!"

"I'm sure I will. I adore you, Ellen Jones. I love talking wedding with you."

"I love talking wedding with you, too, but I have to go pack. I've got an early flight and don't want to miss it."

"Okay, Miss Jones. One more kiss and I'll walk you to the door." Luke gives her a kiss she'll remember throughout the Thanksgiving days she'll spend at Callander.

Ellen Goes Home

Ellen is home! Riding through the town of Marshall, Ellen spots the library where Miss Brenda works. Miss Brenda helped Ellen find information about Jonas Stockman, the Revolutionary War soldier buried on Callander land. Ellen has lovely childhood memories of Saturday visits to the library, checking out Nancy Drew books to devour during the upcoming week.

Ellen passes the *Marshall Times-Standard* building where Mr. Henry, lover of photojournalism, encouraged her to pull a stool up to his workbench and learn about photography. Mr. Henry taught Ellen about the types of shots: long, medium, close-up, and extreme close-up. He taught her how to compose her shots. Ellen looks forward to a long visit with Mr. Henry soon.

Then she is on to Callander plantation land. Passing the grist mill, the commissary, and the blacksmith shop, she comes to the familiar row of sharecropper homes with their chimneys poking through the roofs. The last house in the row belongs to Jo Jo's family. Ellen waves to Jo Jo's mother, who's coming down the steps of her home as they drive past.

Ellen's dad, Will, pulls up to the kitchen door of their home. Amanda, his new wife, is out the door in a flash, reminding Ellen of all the times she's pulled up to this very door only to have Essie, apron flapping in the wind, rush out to meet her. Essie is in town now, and the family will be at her home for Thanksgiving.

"Ellen, we're so glad you're home," says Amanda, hugging Ellen.

Ellen grins. "I could hardly stand it, waiting to be here. You've got to tell me everything, all I've missed since this summer."

Her father holds the door open, waiting for Ellen and Amanda to pass. "We'll let you get settled first. Come out when you're ready, and we'll tell you everything over a cup of coffee."

Picking up her suitcase, Ellen walks down the hall into her room. It is her sanctuary. Always has been. Her furniture is painted in Forest of Ferns, a soft green paint. Curtains and bedspread in sparkling white. The dresser and bookshelves covered with books and family pictures. All just as she remembered. It is so wonderful to be back home at Callander.

Sitting on her bed, as she has done so often during her life, Ellen opens the bedside table and removes her baby book. Her mother, Charlene, recorded all the landmark moments of Ellen's young life in the book. She smiles to see the date her first tooth popped through, then frowns as she remembers the chickenpox her mother had noted in the baby book.

Ellen slides a thin, worn sheet of paper out of the baby book. On it are the predictions of Old Luella, the soothsayer. All the townspeople go to her for predictions about the lives of their newborn babies. Luella wrote three predictions for Ellen: *You will defend the beauty. You will foil a dictator. You will find the soldier.* Even though all three predictions have already come true, Ellen understands they may repeat during her lifetime. Putting the predictions back where she found them, Ellen closes the drawer. She closes away that part of her life.

Over a cup of coffee, Ellen learns that Essie is preparing the Mitchell House for the family's Thanksgiving dinner. "You know Essie will decorate the house to the nines, and the meal will be fabulous. What you don't know is that Essie has asked me to bring my oyster dressing," says Amanda.

Ellen laughs out loud, remembering when Amanda first appeared on the family doorstep. Essie and Amanda did not agree on much of anything. Will had to settle an argument between the two, over having Essie's cornbread dressing or Amanda's oyster dressing for their first Thanksgiving together. How things have changed!

"Julio comes in tomorrow. Rumor has it he's bringing a girl," says Will.

"Heavens!" says Ellen, remembering the boy she picked up in Miami—that brave boy who had flown on a plane from Havana to Miami solo. David and Zia flew him out of Cuba to get him away from Castro. What would it be like to see him again?

Amanda continues her report. "And the day before Thanksgiving, your grandfather is serving lunch to everyone on the plantation. He's been barbecuing pigs and goats for days. And making his famous sauce. We all look forward to David Henry's lunch."

"And Zia?" asks Ellen.

"We'll let her tell you the news from Cuba. She's at the plantation house. She's dying for you to come to see her," says Will.

"I'll see her first thing tomorrow," says Ellen. "But for now, I want to sit here, drink coffee with you two, and hear all the news that's fit to tell."

Ellen moves up the steps of the old plantation house that belongs to her grandfather, David Henry Callander. Before she can open the massive front door, Zia opens the door and envelops Ellen in her arms. Ellen smells Zia's perfume that conjures up the smell of lilies. She feels Zia's wispy hair falling against her cheeks.

"Ellen, finally you're here. Oh, my goodness, it's wonderful to see you!"

Ellen kisses Aunt Zia on the cheek and hugs her in reply.

"I thought you'd like to walk to Jonas' grave. We can talk on the way," says Zia.

"Of course. It's our thing," says Ellen.

"Just let me get my sweater, and we'll go."

While Zia goes to get her sweater, Ellen explores the old plantation house. David Henry Callander's study is on her left with its grand shelves lining the room. The formal parlor with velveteen sofas and oil paintings of ancestors is on Ellen's right. Further down the hall, David Henry's bedroom is on the left and a guest room is on the right. At the end of the vast hallway on the left is the formal dining room with Zia's bedroom on the right. Walking out of the hall onto the back porch, Ellen spots the kitchen. It's separated from the house for practical reasons, to keep the cooking smells out of the living areas and as a precaution in the event of a kitchen fire.

"Ellen, where are you?

"On the back porch. Just checking out the house. You know I love it."

"I know you do. I love it, too. I'd be perfectly happy to live here if David was with me." Zia walks down the broad back steps into the yard with Ellen following close behind. Stepping over the fallen chestnuts, walnuts, and pecans, Ellen catches up and twines Zia's fingers through hers.

"What have you heard from David?" asks Ellen.

"Health-wise, he's fine, though he stresses over Carlota's situation."

"Any news on Carlota?"

"David knows she's with the Literacy Movement. He thought he'd narrowed down her location to a village in Cienfuegos, but when he arrived, the red flag of literacy was flying in the village. The village was literate, so the Literacy Movement workers had moved on to their next location. David went to the adjoining villages. He searched for days but didn't find her.

"Was he able to prove Carlota had been in this village in Cienfuegos?"

"Yes. David took Carlota's picture to show the villagers, and one family certified she'd lived with them for months. They spoke highly of her."

"No complaining about lack of art galleries and concerts?"

Zia laughed. "You remember her visit to Callander. She informed the family gathered around the table over dinner that she couldn't live where no art gallery existed."

Ellen laughed, too. "Carlota succeeded in insulting Essie. Essie, like the rest of us, loves Marshall and Callander with a passion. She was furious over Carlota's snooty attitude."

"Well, if she's working in the fields alongside the peasants, I assume she's lost that snootiness." Turning serious, Zia added, "I hate that she's keeping David from me. She is, you know."

Squeezing Zia's hand, Ellen says, "We'll pray for the safety of them both. I know you, and I know how you worry."

"Yes, but I have you to distract me now. We're going to have a wonderful Thanksgiving."

"Yes, we are. Look, we're almost at Jonas' grave."

"Doesn't it seem strange? We don't have to invent stories about Jonas anymore."

Jonas Stockman fought in the Revolutionary War. His grave stands alone on Callander plantation land. Besides his name, the dates of his birth and death, and the fact that he was a Revolutionary War soldier, Jonas' grave has only the phrase "Truth and Honor" engraved on it.

For more years than Ellen can remember, Ellen and Zia had stood at Jonas' grave and speculated on who he was and why he was buried here, on Callander land. Ellen discovered from records she found in an old trunk that Jonas had come to Marshall in the early 1800s to set up a law practice. The town had turned against him when he testified for an American Indian accused of murder. Jonas was alone when he died, and Ellen's ancestors had buried him on Callander land.

Mystery solved!

Ellen had adopted "Truth and Honor" as her mantra. Ever since she found the wooden desk sign with those words inscribed on it at the bottom of Jonas' trunk and claimed it as her own, those words have guided her. Ellen was the first to break the silence that always seemed to fall upon them when they visited this place.

"I admire Jonas so much," she says. "I guess I'm glad we know who he was and why he's here. I confess I miss our stories. It was so much fun to invent them."

"I feel the same way," says Zia. They stand for a few moments more in silence, paying tribute to this honorable man who fought in the Revolutionary War and once lived in nearby Marshall.

On their way back to the plantation house, Ellen asks Zia about her time with Luke during their visit to Columbia. "Luke was thrilled you took him with you to interview the Brigade 2506 members. Would you tell me about the interviews?"

"Of course, but let me get my notes. We'll get some coffee and sit on the porch. I'd love to share it with you."

Brigade 2506

Ellen and Zia settle in the rocking chairs on the front porch of Callander, coffee in hand. The coffee, with its nut-like aroma of toasted pecans, is Zia's favorite. Ellen wraps both hands around the cup and breathes in the nutty smell.

"Before we start, let me make sure I understand what or who Brigade 2506 is," says Ellen. "Eisenhower authorized the formation of the Brigade from a group of Cuban exiles who lived in Miami. Their purpose was to invade Cuba and defeat Castro. The CIA trained these men. Am I right?"

"That's correct," says Zia.

"And the men you interviewed were part of the Brigade?"

"One was. The other was an American sailor who was part of the invasion."

"What a coup. How on earth did you find these men?"

"I can't tell you. I have to protect the identity of these men and won't tell anyone, even you, who they are and how I found them."

"And you trusted Luke enough to take him with you?"

"Yes, I trust Luke. Plus, I welcomed another professional. The information we received is mind-boggling. I trust you understand you cannot repeat what I tell you."

"Of course. Are you hesitant to air the story when it's finished?"

"Not at all. It's a story that needs to be told. Of primary concern is the identity of my sources and their anonymity."

"Only you and Luke have that information?"

"Correct." Zia took another sip of coffee then began. "Now, in a nutshell, here's the story of the invasion of the Bay of Pigs. The attack was to take place in three phases.

Phase One: Destroy Castro's combat aircraft. Strikes were to take place at three locations.

Phase Two: Take out any remaining combat aircraft belonging to Castro.

Phase Three: Invade Cuba by sea and air.

Here's the kicker, Ellen. The invasion was to take place at Trinidad, a site chosen because it was an anti-Castro town with counter-revolutionary groups. The beach was easy to defend, and the Escambray Mountains nearby offered an escape for Brigade members if they needed one."

"But what happened? Why was the location changed?"

"Kennedy's main concern was that American involvement never be revealed. For some reason, he was concerned about the Trinidad location and, just one month before the invasion, ordered an alternative location to be found."

"And the Bay of Pigs was chosen?"

"Unfortunately, yes. The problem with this location was that the Bay of Pigs was Castro's favorite place to fish, and the local people loved him. Another problem was that the largest swamp in Cuba surrounds the Bay of Pigs, so any other Cubans wanting to join in the revolt could not."

"What a disaster," says Ellen.

"And it gets worse. After the first phase of the operation was completed Kennedy called off phase two. The Brigade 2506 pilots were taxiing for takeoff when they received the news to abort. This action left Castro with combat aircraft. The same planes that Kennedy refused to destroy wreaked havoc on Brigade members.

What's more, during the landing, coral reefs were an unexpected problem. Many of the Brigade members lost their weapons and vital equipment before they reached the shore. When they did reach the shore, they immediately had to fight Cuban soldiers waiting for them. Members of the Cuban Army far outnumbered the Brigade 2506 members on that shore, and the Cuban planes that survived the Brigade attack were firing on them from above. Some of the equipment dropped from our planes sank in the swamp.

Three-quarters of the handful of surviving Brigade members ended up in Cuban prisons. The USS Eaton saved my contact's life. I wish I could convey to you the emotion he displayed when telling me about his rescue. He was treated with great love by the crew members of the Eaton—something he'll never forget."

"There were American ships there at the Bay of Pigs?" asks Ellen.

"Two American Navy destroyers, the USS Eaton and the USS Murray. After Kennedy withdrew support, the invasion began to quickly fail. The Brigade members tried to hide or escape. The sea provided one of the few options for escape. The two American destroyers tried to rescue men in the water and on the beaches, but Castro's forces arrived at the beach and fired on the Eaton, preventing this ship from approaching for a rescue."

Zia fumbled in her notes to find the section she wanted. "These are the sailor's exact words: '*The USS Eaton was extremely close to the beaches when Castro's forces arrived. The ship was in the process of search and rescue for survivors and removing deceased men floating in the water. We were lucky that Castro's forces were not accurate with their shelling of the Eaton, as none hit us, but the bombs were landing all around us and falling from above us as we vacated the area at high speed—speed which takes time to reach when a ship is dead in the water, having stopped to lift small boats and people out of the water. Shells were landing in our wake even as we finally got away from the coastline.*'"

"What an amazing story the sailor tells," says Ellen.

"Yes. But let's back up. The sailor's story starts with the aircraft carrier USS Essex and its task force of destroyers on their way from Norfolk, Virginia, to the Caribbean to conduct ASW exercises."

"ASW exercises?"

Laughing, Zia says, "I had to ask, too. It means Anti-Submarine Warfare exercises. Off the coast of Jacksonville, Florida, the Essex launched the planes used in ASW exercises, and they didn't return. Jet fighters and bomber aircraft landed instead. Our sailor was on a destroyer, the USS Eaton, that pulled up alongside the Essex to refuel, when he saw a strange sight: all aircraft markings were being sanded off the planes. Even more curious, our sailor witnessed seven destroyers forming up in a line to begin a high-speed run.

The Eaton and the Murray, being the fastest two of the destroyers, were ordered to stop dead in the water. The hull numbers, stern name and numbers, stack insignia, and any other identifying marks were painted over. The American flag was taken down. The USS Eaton became a floating gray ship. Nothing remained to identify the USS Eaton as American. At this point, as you can well imagine, the sailors on board the ships were asking themselves, 'What the hell?'"

The Master at Arms—the equivalent to a Chief of Police aboard a Navy ship—ordered the sailors to turn in their cameras. Cameras were confiscated and tagged to be returned to the sailors at a later date.

"The same thing happened on the Murray?" asks Ellen.

"Yes. Late one evening, the Eaton and the Murray rendezvoused with merchant ships—ships that transferred personnel dressed in combat camouflage clothing aboard."

"Brigade members?"

"Yes," says Zia.

"Amazing thing, the sailor I interviewed was on the bridge of the Eaton during the invasion. The bridge was where he worked. All hands were frozen at their duty stations and were not relieved by the next shift, as usual."

"The sailor was not harmed?"

"No." Zia shuffles the pages of her notes. "Listen to this, Ellen."

Zia reads aloud:

During the entire operation and the attempted rescue of survivors, I was on the bridge of the destroyer, observing and listening to everything as it happened. That means I was standing close to the ship's commanding officer and squadron commander, as well as leaders of the brigade, who too had embarked in the middle of the night. Once aboard, there was a total cessation of voice radio using the English language. All communication with the brigade commanders from that point on was in Spanish.

During the Eaton's escape from the beaches, it was feared that shells would hit the ship. Even though the orders were to maintain strict radio silence, the commodore communicated with the aircraft carrier, which was well offshore and out of sight. The carrier immediately told our commodore that he should maintain radio silence, and that any communication was to be encoded. He went straight back in a sternly worded response in plain English to them that we were under intense fire and needed support.

So, another destroyer was sent to our position just in case we were hit while trying to vacate the area. And because this destroyer had not had its hull numbers and U.S. markings removed, it was sighted by the land forces. It's even shown in photographs. The Eaton and its crew were lucky that Castro's tanks, shore batteries, and aircraft were unsuccessful as they bombarded it.

Once the invasion was underway, during the time we were still attempting to rescue survivors, the ship was at battle stations— meaning we were ready for combat and had all gun mounts prepared to fire if ordered to do so. Another reason for being at battle stations is that the entire warship is then completely secured in every compartment, which helps to ensure watertight integrity should incoming fire hit the ship. We were armed and ready, but not permitted to return fire, which would have been easy at that close range.

Zia looked up from her notes.

"Aunt Zia, I envy you, telling these stories to the world. What a responsibility, though, to make sure you truly represent these two men."

"Yes, and I take that responsibility very seriously," says Zia.

Ellen, pushing off the large rocker arms, gets up and walks behind Zia's rocker. Bending over, she kisses the top of Zia's head. Ellen remembers the quote, "Become who you are." Ellen is striving to become her own woman. Along the way, she hopes she becomes like her Aunt Zia.

Thanksgiving Day

Essie, Ellen's aunt on her father's side, wears bibbed aprons, faded now from years of wear. She's never without her laced-up walking shoes, and her salt-and-pepper hair springs from her head in tight curls. Essie is largest around her middle. Her apron strings barely stretch around her to form a bow. Essie is well-versed in the Holy Bible. Amazingly, every conversation with her seems to end in a Bible verse appropriate to the discussion.

Essie came to live with Ellen and her father, Will, after Ellen's mother died. She brought good Southern cooking along with a busyness that kept things flowing and lots of comfort and love into their home. When Will and Amanda married, Essie returned to her home in Marshall.

Essie's home on Nichols Street is something to behold. It's antebellum with four Doric columns reaching from the front porch floor to the roof above the second floor. The stately home is painted white with black, slatted shutters on each side of the two windows on the first floor and the three above, on the second floor. To the right of the two windows on the first floor is the front door, flanked by sidelights of royal blue, cranberry, and bright yellow on each side of the door.

Essie and Will's grandfather, Thomas Brown Mitchell, built the house in the mid-1800s, and it's still known as the Mitchell House. Entering the home, visitors are confronted with an elegant winding staircase leading up to the second floor. To the right of the staircase, a long hall leads to the back of the house. To the left is a large parlor with an equally large dining room just behind the parlor.

The dining room's main attraction is a grand dining table and chairs to seat sixteen made by a local craftsman, Mr. Thomas, who had lived on the Mitchell land. Thomas had followed the Mitchells from South Carolina to Marshall. Ellen remembers holiday meals around the table with family tales woven in with the smells of turkey and ham, fried okra, and homemade desserts.

Ellen can't get to Essie's fast enough. That smell!

Ellen, Will, and Amanda drive up the gravel driveway and park behind the Mitchell House, where Thanksgiving dinner awaits. Getting out of the car, the smells emanating from the kitchen make their collective mouths water. The kitchen of Essie's house, situated a couple of yards from the main house with its unpainted sides and rough steps leading up to the door, stands in sharp contrast to the white, elegant antebellum home.

Ellen can't resist. Walking up the uneven steps, she peers inside and spots the brown turkey with lemons stuffed in its cavity, sweet potatoes still in their jackets, and pecan pies—all on top of the oversized farm table situated in the middle of the room. She walks in, but no one is in the kitchen.

Ellen resists the temptations to pull off part of the turkey to eat as an appetizer. Catching up with Amanda and Will, she walks across the wide back porch into the dining room. Essie is there, putting finishing touches on the already perfect table.

Essie has reinvented the Thanksgiving table she decorated for Thanksgivings spent with Will and Ellen after Ellen's mother died. Two pure white quilts, set on an angle, cover the table. The quilts had belonged to Will and Essie's mother. Plates lining both sides of the table feature the Franciscan wheat pattern, glazed the color of caramel and featuring a shock of wheat in the center of each plate. As a centerpiece, Essie has mixed candles in wooden holders, corn shuck dolls that resemble Pilgrims, and a smattering of small orange, green, and white pumpkins. As has happened so many times before, Ellen silently tells God how thankful she is for Aunt Essie.

Essie has not seen Ellen since she's been home and makes a beeline for her. "Girl, I'm so glad you're home! I've marked off the days. After this feast is over, I'm looking forward to spending some time with you."

"We'll catch up, Aunt Essie. I want to know all the Marshall news about what's been happening in town."

"I look forward to it." Turning as she hears the porch door opening, Essie says, "Look who's here."

Julio walks into the room with an attractive brunette girl in front of him. Here's Julio in Marion Military Academy semi-dress uniform—black dress trousers, black long-sleeve shirt, and black tie. Ellen compares this Julio to the young boy she picked up at Kendall outside of Miami.

Julio is one of the thousands of children sent by Cuban parents to Miami in what is referred to as the Pedro Pan Movement. Parents in Cuba fear the loss of Patria Potestad. Translated, this means "authority of the father." Parents have custody of their children but fear the government will take custody away leaving them with no parental rights over their children. Parents are wise to fear as Castro sent some Cuban children to the Soviet Union to training camps.

This self-assured Julio reminds Ellen that the Julio who left Cuba was brave enough to hide family pictures in his underwear. Cuban soldiers would have taken the photos from Julio had they found him. Just thirteen years old when he left Cuba, Julio is sixteen now.

Everyone in the room talks at once as they shuffle against each other, getting to Julio. Hugs are in order. Ellen quietly walks to the brunette's side. "Hi. I'm Ellen. So glad you could come today."

Relaxing, the girl smiles at Ellen. "I'm Carol. I'm glad to be here with Julio, and I'm glad to meet you. Did you know Julio talks about you all the time?"

Ellen tilts her head to the side and frowns. "Really?"

"Oh, yes. You're one of Julio's favorite people."

"Well, the feeling is mutual. Now, take a deep breath. Everyone will want to meet you and hug you."

Julio speaks up over the happy noise that fills the room. "I want you all to meet Carol. She's a sophomore at Perry County High School in Marion."

As Amanda, Will, and Essie greet Carol, Julio sidles up to Ellen. "Something else to thank you for—making Carol feel welcome."

Ellen turns Julio so that she can give him a tight hug that shows the bond between these two. "Julio, I have missed you. And here you are on a date. I like her, by the way."

"I thought you would, but she still has to pass the Zia test."

"Phooey! You know Zia will love her."

"And, speaking of the devil, or angel in this case, there's Zia. Just look at her, Ellen. Isn't she phenomenal?

"Yes, phenomenal is an excellent word for Zia." Ellen smiles at Julio. Julio smiles back.

"Well, I better go introduce Carol to Zia. Want to go out and find a Christmas tree on Callander land tomorrow? We can get one for your house and Aunt Essie's. You know David Henry already has one picked out for the plantation house."

"Sure. It's one of my favorite things to do."

"Okay. Pick you up around ten o'clock?"

"Yes, I'll be ready. Or come to breakfast with us if you want."

"No, I'll spend time with Zia over breakfast. It will be late when I get back from taking Carol to Marion, and I won't get alone time with Zia today."

Essie breaks in to announce the meal. "Everyone, take your places at the table. We'll have the blessing before we start bringing in the food. Will, saying the blessing falls to you this year."

Ellen gets a hard lump in her throat. Her father will say the perfect blessing for this wonderful family. They hold hands around the table, bow their heads, and listen as Will thanks God for all God has provided.

"Aunt Essie, that was the best Thanksgiving dinner ever," says Ellen.

"Ellen, you say that every year."

Ellen laughs. "It's always true."

"I'm so excited, Ellen. I've got a mystery to show you in the mint julep cabinet," says Essie. "By the way, don't ever taste a mint julep. Nasty stuff!"

Looking around the front parlor, Ellen spots a cabinet with a thick marble top. The mahogany cabinet has a paneled door and its weight rests on scrolled feet. "Is this the mystery cabinet?"

"Yes, it is. Come, let me show you inside." Essie walks over, opens the cabinet door, and pushes aside bourbon bottles. "You'll need to get on your knees to see it best."

Ellen obliges and sees writing in the back of the cabinet. There is a record of the marriage of Mary Ellen Davis and Thaddeus Baird in May 1866.

"Okay, you see that, Ellen: Mary Ellen would have been fifteen years old in May of 1866, as she was born in October of 1850. Mary Ellen Davis married Thaddeus Baird in May of 1866. Now, look at this," Essie says.

Ellen stands to take the worn leather family Bible from Essie. The Bible is open to the section where births, marriages, and deaths are recorded. Ellen's eyes follow line after line of recorded marriages, beautifully written in perfectly slanted cursive letters. There it is— the marriage of Mary Ellen Davis to *Thomas Brown Mitchell*—not Thaddeus Baird—in December of 1866.

"No mention of Thaddeus Baird in the Bible?"

"As you can see, just Thomas Mitchell."

"How could Mary Ellen marry one man in May and another in December? Ooooh! We've got a mystery on our hands. So, what's next?" Ellen closes the old Bible and hands it back to Essie.

"I've been thinking about that very thing. This house was built in the mid-1800s by Thomas Brown Mitchell, who would have been an older man when Mary Ellen married him. So, this was Mary Ellen's home. I'm sure she lived here until she passed away. I keep thinking maybe there's something of hers here in the house. Old writings or such."

"That sounds reasonable. Have you searched?"

"There's nothing in the living part of the house. I haven't searched in the attic."

"Maybe that's next."

"You're right, but I keep putting it off. It's a little spooky up there."

"We'll do it together. It will have to be during spring break."

"That's fine. Mary Ellen's mystery can wait that long."

"And now I hear Dad calling my name. It's time to head back to Callander." Ellen hugs Essie tightly. "It was the best Thanksgiving ever."

"Go on now. And about our mystery, 'Ask, and it will be given to you; seek, and you will find; knock, and it will be opened to you. Matthew 7:7.'"

Essie adds, "And don't you forget to come to see me before you leave for college."

"I won't, Aunt Essie." Ellen turns and blows a kiss to Essie as she walks out of the parlor into the dining room.

Ellen and Julio

Ellen, Will, and Amanda are lingering around the kitchen table with a second cup of coffee when Julio walks in unannounced.

"Are you ready, Ellen?"

"Let me run to my room and get my coat."

"Do you want a cup of coffee, Julio?" asks Will.

"No, thank you. When Ellen is ready, we'll find a Christmas tree. I need to get to Marion this afternoon."

"Your need to go to Marion has anything to do with Carol?"

"Well, yes, it does. Carol wants me to come to her house for a leftover party."

"That's what I think it is?"

"Yes, probably. Friends and family come to Carol's parents and bring what's left of Thanksgiving with them. Carol says it's great fun. Tons of good food to eat."

"Carol's parents didn't mind her missing Thanksgiving dinner in Marion?"

"I'm sure they did, but they were kind enough to let her come to Marshall with me."

Ellen walks into the kitchen, her right arm in her jacket. Julio walks over and holds her jacket so she can put her left arm in. Ellen nods thanks to Julio and says, "We'll see you two later. Don't worry if it takes us a while. You know we want the perfect tree. Forgot to tell you, Julio. Essie doesn't need one. We're just getting a tree for our house."

"Yes, ma'am," says Julio, stopping to pick up an ax by the back door as they walk out of the house. "Goodbye, Will and Amanda. I'll see you before I go back to school."

"I'm glad we had some time alone, Ellen. I'm worried about Carlota and need someone to talk to about her. You're it," says Julio.

"I'm not surprised you're worried about Carlota. Of course, I'll listen."

"She's involved with a man, you see."

"And David knows about this?"

"No. Carlota would not bring this man home to meet Daddy. A guerrilla fighter, he was with Castro as far back as when Batista was in power. He was part of a group involved in a guerrilla campaign against Batista in the Sierra Maestra mountains. The group called themselves the 26th of July Movement. Their activities expanded, disrupting the Cuban economy. The group burned sugar cane plantations. Their bombings in Havana all but stopped the tourist trade. This guerrilla group still fights for Castro."

"I can see why David would be worried about him being in Carlota's life. She's written to you?"

"Oh, yes. Carlota's fallen head-over-heels in love with Castro's movement and, since this guerrilla fighter is a part of Castro's movement, she thinks she's in love with him as well."

"You know Carlota is head-strong. I don't know what you can do to change her thinking."

"Oh, I know I can't do that. That's not my problem. Carlotta's begging me not to tell Zia or David. According to her, she wants me to share in her happiness."

"Julio, you have to make your own decision about this."

"I know, Ellen, but how can I *not* tell Zia and David? What if something happens to her?"

"I think you've just solved your problem, Julio. Tell Zia. She'll find a way to tell David."

"You're right, Ellen. I don't know if Dad can do anything, but at least I will have warned him."

"That's a heavy load you've been carrying. Do you feel better now?"

"I'll always worry about Carlota, but, yes, I feel better just knowing what I'm going to do." Julio grins, "Now, let's find your perfect tree. I need to get to Marion."

Ellen watches Julio as he begins walking through the sagebrush. She loves him, this young man who is a survivor and a brother. That's what he is to Ellen. She rushes to catch up with him. Grinning up at him, she tucks her arm in his.

"Look, Julio. Through the bushes. Do you see it?" asks Ellen.

"It looks like an old church."

"It is. According to Granddaddy Callander, it was built in the early 1800s."

Ellen and Julio walk closer to the church. Part of the roof has fallen, and the few remnants of paint left show that the church was once painted white. The large front door is arched, and the single windows on each side of the door are arched as well.

"Come on, Julio. Let's go inside. I want to show you something."

"I'm not going in there."

"Oh, come on, you ninny," says Ellen. She walks up the concrete steps that lead to the front door. Pushing the door open, Ellen walks inside. Julio pauses a moment, then walks in behind Ellen.

"This is what I want you to see. See all these holes about the size of quarters? They're all over the floor."

Bending down, Julio looks at the holes.

"Granddaddy told me this church was part of the Underground Railroad. Runaway slaves were held under the church until it was safe to get them to the next stop on the Railroad. The holes were drilled in the floor to help the slaves breathe."

"Wow, Ellen. Imagine how terrified the slaves were. Just the way I felt leaving Cuba by myself."

Ellen puts an arm around Julio's shoulders and squeezes. They stand for a moment, and Ellen imagines out loud what the church would have looked like with a choir singing in the choir loft, a preacher standing behind the pulpit, and the church pews filled with people dressed in their church finery. Ellen can almost hear them singing "In the Garden."

Ellen moves first. "Okay, Julio. Let's go. Daylight's wasting."

Walking out of the church, Julio spots a cedar tree off to the right of the church. Pointing, Julio asks, "What about that tree, Ellen?"

Walking over to the cedar, Ellen circles the tree, inspecting it more closely. The trunk of the tree is straight, and it's the right height.

"It's perfect, Julio. Let's cut it down."

After chopping down the tree and hoisting it over his shoulder, Julio follows Ellen home. He smiles as he hears Ellen humming the tune of the old hymn, "In the Garden."

Jo Jo and Ilenia

A montage of images from her Thanksgiving visit merge and flow through Ellen's mind: dinner at the Mitchell House, Essie and the mint julep cabinet, Julio and Carol, porch time with Zia, conversation with her father and Amanda as they decorated the tree. So much love. So much gratitude for such a family welled up in her as she gazed out the airplane window, now on her way back to Miami.

Ellen's thoughts turn to Luke—what she feels for him and all the questions she has about a marriage with him. What will it be like to meet his parents? Where will they make their home? Are there children in their future? How will they balance their respective careers and a life that's shared?

Then Jo Jo. Ellen had deep feelings for Jo Jo in high school. Were they the same as what she feels for Luke now? It's very messy, sorting through your feelings, she realizes just before she nods off for a quick nap before the plane touches down in Florida.

As Ellen walks up the steps to Caldwell Hall, Miss Nancy opens the front door to greet her. Miss Nancy, with her permed hair, her swing skirt with pumpkins around the hem, and, today, orange loafers to match. Ellen smiles. She's glad to see Miss Nancy, the guardian of the girls in Caldwell Hall and a steady presence in their lives.

"Ellen, you're the first one back. I'm so glad you're home."

Ellen realizes Caldwell Hall is home for Miss Nancy. She feels sad that Miss Nancy doesn't have a large family that loves and supports her, no place to return for the holidays.

"Miss Nancy, it's so good to see you. Has it been quiet around here with all of us gone?"

"Yes, except for the fact that Amelia's mother has put up a Christmas tree in your room. Miss Caroline took it upon herself to decorate the tree with ornaments that represent the fifty states of the USA. And she brought me some deviled eggs with peanut butter in the mix."

Ellen throws her shoulders back and laughs out loud.

"Laugh if you will. Just wait until you see the tree in your room. Oh, and I have something for you—a letter from that young man in Africa. I thought I'd best keep it. I wouldn't put it past Miss Caroline to read it if I left it in your room."

Miss Nancy hurries down the hall to the left to get the letter from her room and returns with the familiar blue envelope. What tales would Jo Jo have to tell in this letter from across the world? Ellen takes the letter from Miss Nancy and kisses her on the cheek.

"It's good to see you, Miss Nancy."

"Thank you, dear. It's good to see you, too. You're the first back, but the rest will start trickling in throughout the day."

Ellen is glad for the quietness as she puts her suitcase down and settles on the bed with Jo Jo's letter.

Dear Ellen,

It seems like ages since we've written to each other. I keep all your letters and read them over and over again

The most exciting thing to happen here is Ilenia invited me to have dinner with her family. She picked me up on the base, and we drove to her home in Garden City. Garden City is an upscale neighborhood where the elite of Libya live. Ilenia's house is a two-storied stucco with a flat roof, and it's surrounded by what I'd guess is a ten-foot stucco fence. Palm trees everywhere and brightly colored flowers in full bloom.

Her mother, who stays home and keeps house, was friendly enough. She served traditional Libyan food at the meal. The soup, served first, was a lamb and tomato soup called shorba. We then had a delicious beef, pumpkin, and caramelized onion dish. My favorite was fried dates with bsisa. It's made with ingredients that include ground chickpeas, coriander seeds, and olive oil.

Ilenia's father was another story. I understand that he's a lawyer and a prosperous one. I admit I was nervous talking with him. I was so relieved when dinner was over! He was very stiff and made me uncomfortable.

After dinner with her family, Ilenia wanted to show me another side of Tripoli. We drove out of the city toward the countryside.

About two kilometers out of town, on the right side of the two-lane road, was a huge garbage dump. As we approached it, Ilenia tells me to look closely at the dump. Turns out Arabs were living in the garbage dump and had made the large cardboard boxes their home. It haunts me. I've never seen poverty like this.

A couple more kilometers down the road, I see the shells of concrete buildings—walls standing with no rooftops. Ilenia tells me they're from World War II. Even with no ceilings, the buildings would be better to live in than the garbage dump. Ilenia says the Arabs are very superstitious. It would be very unlucky to live in these ruins left over from the war. Funny thing! The Arabs build stick huts leaning on World War II buildings. That's okay, as long as they don't live inside.

Remember Rommel, the Desert Fox? Hitler sent Rommel and the Afrika Korps to North Africa to shore up the Italian forces who were having a hard time winning against the British. Rommel wound up commanding the entire North African Campaign. He fascinates me, even though he was on the wrong side of the war. Rommel was falsely accused of plotting to assassinate Hitler, and Hitler gave Rommel a choice between suicide or facing a trial for treason. Rommel committed suicide by taking cyanide. Bet you didn't know that!

Later on our drive, there were groves of oranges, stretching as far as the eye can see, such a welcome sight after all the ghosts of World War II. Ilenia pulled the car off the road and, plucking two oranges off a tree, she peeled the oranges and handed me one. We sat in the car, eating these fabulous oranges with juice dripping down off our chins. We laughed so hard.

We would have run into the edge of the Sahara if we had continued down that road. Not a lot of kilometers between the Mediterranean and the Sahara. I enjoy this country and know Ilenia makes the difference. She's showing me parts of Libya I probably wouldn't see on my own. She says we're going dancing at the Uaddan this weekend. Built in 1935, it's the oldest hotel in Tripoli. I hear it's luxurious; you have to wear a coat and tie to go in. Sophia Loren has a suite at the Uaddan. Wouldn't that be something? To see Sophia Loren.

At the Uaddan, service members mostly play roulette in the casino or hang out in the lounge with the British and oil company people. There's a five-hundred-seat theatre, too. The owners of the Uaddan bring in actors and musicians that appeal to Westerners. I'm looking forward to it. The food will be exotic, but I'm most excited about dancing. Ilenia says there's a nice-sized dance floor and a band will be playing some American music.

Well, I'd better get this in the mail. Let me hear from you.

Jo Jo

Ellen absorbs Jo Jo's letter. Considering she and Luke are talking about marriage, Jo Jo's letter about Ilenia should not bother her. But it does. Ellen's not proud of herself for feeling this way. What's that phrase? You cannot have your cake and eat it, too?

Find a picture of the Uaddan is in Ellen's Notebook at the end of the book.

Luke and Sandra

Ellen and Sandra are working on news stories in the broadcasting workspace that doubles as a classroom. Luke comes in and waltzes over to Ellen, kissing her on the top of her head.

"What ya working on, Cotton?" asks Luke.

"A story about Miami's…"

"Hey, Luke, will you read this for me? I have less than thirty minutes to file this story for today's show," says Sandra.

"Sure," says Luke, walking to Sandra's table.

Ellen tries to keep the irritation she feels off her face.

"I couldn't decide whether to write about the Freedom Riders who were attacked by a white mob at a bus station in McComb, Mississippi, or Enos, the chimpanzee who was launched into space yesterday," says Sandra

"And you chose?" asks Luke

"Enos. His launch is part of NASA's Project Mercury. Enos orbited the earth twice—he's the first chimpanzee to do that," says Sandra.

"Let's see what ya got," says Luke. Sandra hands Luke her typed story.

Luke reads the story:

On November 29, Enos was the first chimpanzee to orbit the earth. Russian cosmonauts, Yuri Gagarin and Gherman Titov, achieved orbit in April before Enos. Enos' achievement sets the stage for an American astronaut to orbit Earth.

NASA trained Enos for the flight by having him manipulate controls on the spacecraft where lights flashed. The chimpanzee was rewarded with banana pellets when he responded correctly, and he received a shock on his feet when he answered incorrectly. In-flight equipment malfunctioned, and, despite responding correctly, Enos received seventy-six shocks to his feet.

Enos survived the shock treatment to run around the deck of the recovery ship after his rescue from the landing pod. Enos shook hands with his rescuers.

Once again, Enos, the first American American chimpanzee in space, has successfully orbited Earth twice.

"Ouch. I hate to hear about Enos being shocked. Seems inhumane to me," says Luke

"I know. I feel the same way," says Sandra. "So, I'm good to go with the story?"

"Except for one thing. In your conclusion, you write that Enos was the first American chimpanzee in space, and that's not true," says Luke.

"What?"

"Look, I follow most stories about NASA, and I know Ham the chimpanzee was launched into space in January. Ham was the first chimp in space, not Enos."

Sandra looks at her watch. "Luke, I've got five minutes to get this story to the control room. I'm pushing it. I can't change it now 'cause I'd have to retype the whole story. Dr. Shelby won't accept a script that's not perfect. I can't just strike that sentence out."

"What are you going to do?"

"I'm filing it as is, and I hope no one catches my mistake."

"I'd probably do the same. Now run, before Dr. Shelby has your head."

Luke makes his way back to Ellen's desk, smiling about Sandra's dilemma. He drops the smile when he sees Ellen's face.

"What's wrong, Ellen?"

"You. Sometimes I think I don't know you."

"What'd I do?"

"You encouraged Sandra to file a story with incorrect information."

"What else could she do?"

"She could have explained to Dr. Shelby. He could have worked something out. She's discredited our entire program by deliberately filing incorrect information."

"You know, Ellen. Sometimes I think I don't know you."

Without a word, Ellen gathers her papers and stomps out of the workroom.

Seeking refuge in her dorm room, Ellen paces the floor, feeling torn about her feelings for Luke. Ellen has never seen a chink in his professionalism before, but she sure saw a huge chink today. Does he really feel it's okay to file incorrect information just to meet a deadline?

Ellen stops pacing in front of her desk with its family pictures and Jonas Stockman's wooden desk sign. She picks up the sign and stares at the words. *Truth and Honor*. They mean everything to Ellen, but what do they mean to Luke?

Ellen hears the familiar tapping on the dorm window and knows it's Luke. She struggles to raise the massive window, not certain she even wants to speak to the man she's not sure she knows at all anymore.

"I know you're in there pacing the floor," says Luke. "You think I'm an unprofessional jerk."

"Close," says Ellen, frowning down at this man she plans to marry.

"I know you're disappointed in me. I want you to know the Enos story was mine to deliver on the show. I left out the phrase: *the first American chimpanzee in space*. I wanted you to know."

"Good. I can stop worrying about Dr. Shelby. He gives so much to the broadcasting program, and incorrect information on a show would devastate him. I'm glad you didn't let that happen. But what about Sandra?"

"I told her to talk to Dr. Shelby but, knowing her, she'll never admit she left incorrect information in her story."

"So, what happens?"

"She was retyping the story when I left. I assume she'll swipe the original story and put the retyped story in with the show's other news stories."

"So, Dr. Shelby will grade the second script?"

"I'll just bet that's what will happen."

"That bothers me," says Ellen. "What's to stop her from doing it again?"

"I'll talk to her, Ellen. I swear to you. Look, nothing happened. No incorrect information went out." Ellen frowns but doesn't say a word.

"Ellen, I've been thinking. I know you're right, and this could have been a really bad situation. But it's over. Now, come on. Let's move on. I love you. Don't stay mad at me."

Luke leans in the window and kisses Ellen. She kisses him back. It's hard to stay mad at Luke the Legend.

"Gotta run, Ellen. You know I love ya," says Luke.

"I love you, too," says Ellen, but the frown is back on her face as she watches Luke run down the dorm steps and speed across campus.

DECEMBER 1961

Mr. Chenard

Detective Wofford of Coral Gable's Police Department smiles at Ellen as she walks into the department. "There's our girl. Mr. Chenard is back in the conference room. You know the way."

"Good morning, Detective. Solving the crimes of Coral Gables today?"

"As ever."

Ellen grins at the detective and moves confidently down the hall toward the conference room. As she enters the room, Mr. Chenard stands. Ellen remembers that it's been almost three weeks since she's seen the dignified Cuban refugee.

Echoing her thoughts, Mr. Chenard says, "I have missed your visits, Ellen. How was your family?

"Wonderful. Magical. You must meet my family one day, Mr. Chenard."

"I look forward to that. It will be my pleasure to meet your family."

Ellen slides a wooden chair toward the table to face Mr. Chenard and sits down. She leans forward.

"Have you thought about the Peabody? About my writing your story and entering it in competition?"

Ellen takes in her breath and holds it, not sure at all of Mr. Chenard's answer.

"You may use my story. My wife says I need to tell how it is in our Cuba today."

Ellen's breath seeps out, and she sits back, relieved and honored. "I am humbled, Mr. Chenard."

"So, let us begin." Mr. Chenard pushes his wire-rimmed glass up on his nose with his index finger. "My wife, Louisa, is the center of my world. She's a small dove of a woman who loves me. Unfortunately, her father is related to Osvaldo Dorticós Torrado, the current president of Cuba. I believe they are first cousins."

"And this relationship interfered with your life?"

"It is good for Louisa's family; they want for nothing. It was bad for me. I could not keep quiet about Castro. I told you before how we teachers were restricted in what we could teach our students. Castro's goal was to educate the people by teaching socialism and to create a literate population loyal to him. I didn't obey. I could not stand between my students and George Orwell's *1984*.

"And you were in danger?"

"Yes. I became a part of the Cuban underground and wrote anti-Castro pamphlets that were distributed all over Havana. Cubans were not allowed to produce or distribute any written word that was not approved by the government."

"And your punishment if you were caught?"

"I could join the twenty thousand dissidents in prison or, I suppose, I could be executed. It was not about me. I was much more concerned about Louisa's fate if Castro captured me."

"So, you left?"

"Yes, and I left behind my heart. Off the subject of Louisa, I wrote a song about liberty. I understand they still sing it in Cuba today. Would you like to hear it?"

Ellen nods. Mr. Chenard sings in a silvery voice—clear and light.

I lie on my back and see the stars—Liberty
I hold my firstborn in my arms—Liberty
I walk with my father to his ancestors' graves—Liberty
I lift my head to the sky and sing—Liberty

The word "liberty" hangs in the air. A single tear rolls down Ellen's cheek. This poignant song of a man's love of country as it once was touches her deeply.

"Your love of Cuba and Louisa touches me so."

"Ah, Ellen, no se puede evitar. It cannot be helped. My Louisa is there. I am here."

"Are you in touch with Louisa?"

"Yes, but we have to be ever so careful. Louisa's family tells anyone who asks that we are divorced and that she wants no contact with me. We mail our letters to a friend of mine at the university. I could never write to her at her home."

"But you're not divorced."

"No. Louisa loves me. I mail poems and stories of America to her. She writes of everyday family events but makes no mention of Castro or the movement. My prayer is one day the evil bastard, Castro, will leave our beautiful country. Then I can go home. To hold my Louisa. To walk up the steps to the university and see the frescoes dedicated to medicine, science, art, philosophy, liberal arts, literature, and law—stunning they are. To sit in an outdoor café with old friends, the Cuban Spanish blending with the cigar smoke swirling around us. Most of all, I miss my Louisa."

Ellen and Mr. Chenard sit in silence. Ellen looks down at the pages of notes she's taken. A heartbreaking story reduced to words on a page. The tears come again.

"Ellen, look at me. Don't feel sad for me. I have freedom. I lift my head to the sky and sing—liberty."

Ellen begins to pack her things. She stands up, still crying a river of tears.

"Come here, Ellen."

Mr. Chenard hands her his handkerchief. "Stop those tears. You finish your story, and we will celebrate. I'll take you to a Cuban party. The party will be in your honor. The journalist with a warm, caring soul."

Ellen Directs

Dr. Shelby, head of the broadcast journalism department, takes his pipe out of his mouth and announces Ellen will be directing the newscast today. This is a first for Ellen, who has long thought directing may be where she belongs. Ellen does not want to be on-air talent, a cameraperson, or a technical operator. She does love editing and reporting, but directing is dangling out there, too, like something exciting yet to be discovered.

Now in the control room, she sits in the tall director's chair, puts on her headset, and asks for sound checks. The floor director relays Ellen's request to Luke and Sandra, interrupting the flirtation going on between the two. Ellen's gut clenches.

"Sandra first. Please read your script until I ask you to stop."

Sandra begins the soundcheck in a low voice.

"Floor director, tell Sandra she has to use her on-air voice or this soundcheck is useless."

The floor director relays the information to Sandra, who immediately begins to read her script at the correct level. The audio technician adjusts the fader to set Sandra's volume.

"Now, Luke."

Sensing Ellen's mood, Luke reads from his script until Ellen says he can stop.

Ellen asks camera one to get a close-up on Luke and camera two to get a two-shot. Camera one has too much headroom on Luke, and Ellen advises the operator to fix the shot. Everything's ready. She cues the audio technician to play opening music and has the technical director, or TD for short, fade into the two-shot. Ellen cues the floor director to start the countdown.

"5, 4, 3..." The floor director holds up his right hand and counts down, then switches to his fingers to motion the final count of 2, 1. The floor director indicates "Go" by performing an exaggerated point to Luke to show he's on air.

Luke and Sandra open the show on the two-shot. Ellen directs the TD to switch to camera one as Luke begins the lead story about Castro's announcement that he would guide Cuba to becoming a socialist state. There will be only one political party in Cuba, The United Party of Cuba's Socialist Revolution.

Switch to camera two. During Luke's story, Ellen has asked camera two to get a close-up on Sandra. Sandra's story involves the United States conducting a nuclear test at the Nevada Test Site.

Switch to camera one. Luke informs the audience that the price of gas has gone up to twenty-seven cents per gallon.

Switch to camera two. Sandra's story is about the birth control pill, now available to the women of Great Britain.

On camera two, Luke tells the viewer that Floyd Patterson knocked out Tom McKeeley to win the heavyweight boxing title.

Ellen asks for a two-shot on camera one and signals the TD to switch cameras. Luke and Sandra close the show.

Ellen directs the TD to put a graphic on the screen and takes the headset off her head. By gosh, she loves it! Directing is exhilarating. You have to think on your feet and be ready to make changes during the show while juggling the control room and studio crew.

Then she thinks of Mr. Chenard. Ellen knows she would never give up reporting for directing. There are too many important stories that need telling, like Mr. Chenard's. Nonetheless, she's going to enjoy this feeling while it lasts.

"Good job, Ellen. We'll make you a director yet," says Dr. Shelby, clamping down on his pipe.

Luke walks into the control room. "Perfect job, Cotton." He leans over and kisses Ellen on the top of her head.

Sandra is still sitting at the anchors' desk, a sour look on her face. She's watching Ellen and Luke through the glass separating the studio from the control room.

Ellen ignores Sandra. All of a sudden, Sandra's attitude and flirtations with Luke don't matter. Sandra doesn't matter.

Ellen did it! She directed, and she feels fabulous.

Ellen Meets Luke's Parents

Ellen's in her dorm room, waiting for Luke and his parents to pick her up at Caldwell Hall. She's nervous. What if she's not bright enough? What if she's not attractive enough? What if she's not good enough for Luke in his parents' eyes? Walking to her desk, she looks down at the pictures of her dad, Aunt Zia, and the Callander plantation house, taking comfort from these pictures of her life.

Curtain call! Miss Nancy comes to tell Ellen she has visitors in the lobby. Grabbing her car coat, Ellen follows Miss Nancy down the wide stairs to the lobby, remembering when she walked down these same steps to meet Amanda for the first time. That turned out okay. Throwing her shoulders back, Ellen thinks this meeting will be just fine as well.

There's Luke with that charming grin on his face. No nerves there. Standing beside him is a tall, gangly man in a dress shirt and tie. At least fifteen keys are threaded on a silver circle attached to Luke's father's belt with a leather strap. Ellen assumes these are the keys to various doors at the theaters Luke's father owns. Is he wearing them out of habit? Did he forget to leave them at home? Ellen has no way of knowing.

Breaking the silence, Luke's mother says, "Ellen, we're thrilled to meet you." She grabs both of Ellen's hands and pumps them.

"As usual, Mother, you've beaten me to the punch." Putting his arm around his mother's shoulders to show he means no offense, Luke says, "Yes, this is Ellen Jones. Ellen, meet my father, William, and my mother, Elaine."

"I'm pleased to meet you both. Luke and I are so glad that you're here. How long will you be here?" *Damn. Now they'll think I can't wait for them to leave.* Ellen silently chastises herself.

"Just two days. I have to get back to the theaters on Sunday," says Luke's dad.

"Well, we can cram a lot into two days. We'll start with dinner in Coral Gables. Do you want to go to the Italian restaurant we went to last time you were in town?" asks Luke.

"I guess. That restaurant didn't serve Veal Saltimbocca, but I suppose I can order something else," Luke's father says.

"Yes. Let's go there," his mother says. "I loved dining in the courtyard with the fountains splashing. What fun!"

"Okay, then. We're off." Luke leads the way and they pile in the Ford rental car together.

With drinks served and orders placed, Ellen begins to relax.

"Tell me about your parents, Ellen. I assume they're Democrats," says Luke's dad.

Uh, oh! "My father voted for Richard Nixon. Most of the people in our town did."

"And where is home, Ellen?" asks Luke's mother, ignoring the stormy look on the father's face.

Ellen's face brightens. A chance to talk about Callander! Leaving nothing out, Ellen tells them about the plantation and all those who call it home.

"So, you were influenced by your Aunt Zia to pursue broadcasting as a career?" asks Luke's mother.

"Yes. And I understand that you are a journalist. I know you have influenced Luke."

"Maybe initially, but from the time Luke saw his first newscast, he was obsessed. That's what he wanted to do with his life. I'm proud of him. He read news stories aloud, recording them on a reel-to-reel tape recorder. He did this for years until he lost the Southern accent."

Ellen looked at Luke with respect. What an impressive thing for a teenager to do. Ellen turns her attention to Luke's father, who is playing with his Chicken Saltimbocca. "I understand Luke worked for you at the theaters."

"Yes, he did, all through his high school years. I have to say he was a good worker. His senior year in high school, I had to take him out of the ticket booth and make him a projectionist. The girls wouldn't leave him alone. At least they couldn't get to him in the projection room."

Luke grinned at Ellen. "It was that Luke the Legend charm."

Ellen grinned back, thinking of this teenaged Luke she would have loved to have known. Turning down the Tiramisu, the group makes plans for the next day. Luke is taking his parents to visit relatives who live nearby for the day, but Ellen will join them for dinner again tomorrow night. They drive back to Ellen's dorm, where Luke walks her to her door. Before Ellen can say a word, Luke kisses her without a thought of his parents in the car watching.

Ellen is with Luke and his parents at Joe's Stone Crab restaurant. After everyone has ordered the famous crab claws, Luke's father begins the conversation by talking about marriage. "I know I may be jumping the gun, but have you two talked about marriage?"

Ellen doesn't move, much less answer. She's shocked that Luke's father would open this topic before she and Luke are engaged and in a more official position toward marriage.

Luke senses Ellen's discomfort, but answers truthfully. "Ellen and I have talked about marriage. We've discussed having the wedding at Callander, the plantation in Alabama."

The talk of a wedding draws a frown from the father who persists with his questions.

"And where would you live? I assume anywhere you have a job, Luke."

"As you can guess, that's all up in the air. I insist on a job in a major market, so who knows where we'll land."

Ellen says softly, "I'll have another year of college after Luke graduates."

"So, you're saying you'll get married after you graduate, Ellen?" asks Luke's father.

"I want to get married right after I graduate. I don't want to live without this lady." Luke picks up Ellen's hand and kisses it.

"Ellen, I'm sure you'll bow to Luke's wishes. His career is most important. He will go far, you know."

Intuitively, Luke's mother realizes the dilemma facing Luke and Ellen. Luke's father is oblivious to the problem. So that Ellen doesn't have to respond, Luke's mother jumps into the conversation. "We only have males in our family. You can't imagine how thrilled I am at the idea of a daughter."

They finish dessert, and Luke and his father leave the restaurant to bring the car around. Luke's mother takes the opportunity to speak her mind. "Ellen, if you love your journalism work half as much as I do, you need to follow your path as much as Luke needs to follow his. Luke's path should not take you away from your path. I know you and Luke love each other."

"For the record," she says, "I badly want you in the family. I admire everything I've heard about you. In the end, you two have important decisions to make. I know this sounds strange coming from Luke's mother, but a marriage shouldn't be built on sacrifice. You two must figure it out."

As Ellen and Luke's mother stand, Ellen turns and hugs Luke's mother fiercely. Ellen pulls back and looks Elaine in the eye. "Thank you."

A Piña Colada Salad

Ellen walks into the dorm room and sniffs. "What's that odor, Amelia?"

"I hope you're smelling the air freshener and not my cigarette smoke. Does it smell like pine trees?" asks Amelia.

"First of all, what the heck is air freshener?"

Amelia walks over to her desk and picks up the bottle. "See. Just pull this ring, and a wick pops up out of the bottle and… voilà. Instant pine fragrance. No more cigarette smoke."

"Amelia, we have talked and talked about your smoking. I don't think it's good for you, and you have to think about your image. Do you know what they say at Callander? Girls that smoke will drink. Girls that drink will do anything."

"You're such a stick in the mud, Ellen. And I suppose by 'anything' you mean sex. Well, I just might—have sex I mean. If I ever find the right boy. I think back seat bingo might be fun."

"You're just trying to shock me. What happened to Roger?"

"Oh, I caught him with that awful Betty Johnson, so that's over."

"Well, I'm sure the right guy is out there, but he won't be crazy about your smoking."

"It's not my fault, Ellen. The university makes it too easy."

"And tell me how the University of Columbus is responsible for your smoking."

"It is! The university allows representatives from the cigarette companies to stand outside our campus cafeteria and give out cigarette samples. You've seen them. Little boxes with four cigarettes inside. Free for the taking. That's how I started. It's the university's fault."

"I do see your point, but someone representing the university is not putting that cigarette in your mouth and lighting it."

"Give it up, Ellen. I'll stop when I'm ready."

"Fine, but no boy wants to kiss a dirty ashtray."

"Okay, okay. I see your point. Enough talk about cigarettes. Do tell all about Luke's parents."

"His father is abysmal, but his mother almost makes up for the father."

"You like her, huh?"

"Yes, and respect her. The whole issue of Luke's career versus my career came up. The abysmal father implied that my career is of no significance, only Luke's career matters. Luke's mother told me to follow my path."

"Well, that's unusual in a future mother-in-law."

"Elaine—that's her name—is a journalist. She understands me."

"So, the question is, what are you going to do about marrying Luke?"

"I'm going to take his mother's advice and follow my path. I'm going to graduate with a degree in journalism from this university. Then we'll see where my path takes me."

"Good girl, Ell…"

"What is that awful smell?" says Miss Caroline as she enters the dorm room, purse in her left hand and a plate balanced in her right hand.

"Hello, Mother. It's polite to knock, you know."

"Oh, I know you girls are always glad to see me. Plus, I've brought you a treat."

"That white and yellow squiggly thing?" asks Amelia

"Yes, it's Piña Colada Salad."

"Yum," says Amelia, sarcastically.

"I think it does look yummy," says Ellen as she takes a closer look. It's a white gelatin ring with the yellow of pineapple pieces showing here and there. Miss Caroline has filled the center of the ring with chunks of pineapple topped with long shreds of coconut.

"I knew you girls would like it."

With a change of heart, Amelia digs out three plates, pink plastic with roses on them, and some spoons from her center desk drawer. "Come on, Mother. Sit on my bed, and I'll serve the salad. It does look good."

Thrilled at this chance to socialize with the girls, Miss Caroline wiggles out of her wool coat and sits down. "Now, what is that smell?"

Changing the subject, Ellen says, "Let's talk about movies. I can't wait to see *Pocket Full of Miracles*. It comes out next week. Bette

Davis plays a beggar woman named Apple Annie, who is turned into a lady of high society with the help of local gangsters. Apple Annie's daughter, played by Ann-Margret, is marrying into royalty. She brings the royal family to New York to meet Apple Annie, who has convinced her daughter that she's a society lady, not a beggar."

"That sounds okay. My favorite movie this year is *Come September* because I adore Bobby Darin," says Amelia.

"Ellen, I thought you'd want to see *Blue Hawaii* with Elvis Presley," says Miss Caroline.

"No Elvis movies for me. I love his music, but I'm not crazy about his movies," says Ellen.

"So, which movies do you think will be nominated for the Academy Award this year?" asks Amelia. "I think *A Raisin in the Sun* with Sidney Poitier will be a nominee, for sure."

"Well, for once we agree, Amelia. I'll add *The Hustler* with Paul Newman to the list," says Miss Caroline.

"And I agree with both of you and add *Judgment at Nuremberg* to the list. In this film, four German judges who were on the bench during the Nazi's rule are tried for crimes against humanity. Funny thing—our lead story today on *Miami News Now* was about Adolph Eichmann," says Ellen. "Today, Eichmann was found guilty of crimes against the Jews during World War II."

"Wasn't he the Nazi responsible for deporting the Jews to those killing centers where the Nazis gassed the Jews?" says Miss Caroline.

"Yes," says Ellen. "The thing that is so right about this story is that Eichmann was tried in Jerusalem."

"I'll bet they'll hang him," says Amelia.

"I'll guess we'll find out in a few days when the Jerusalem court sentences him."

Standing up, Miss Caroline picks up her purse. "I've enjoyed this girl time, but I've got to run. Bridge is at my house tonight. I'm leaving the Piña Colada Salad with you. Don't forget to refrigerate it. It's sure to be a sloppy mess if you don't."

Shocking Ellen, Amelia gets up and hugs her mother. "Thank you for visiting, Mother."

"We enjoyed the salad, Miss Caroline," says Ellen.

"You'd probably rather have the real thing, but I can't help you with that," says Miss Caroline.

"Mother!" says Amelia, faking a shocking reply.

"And don't you worry. I know how much you love my deviled eggs. I'll bring those next time. Bye, you two darlings," says Miss Caroline as she goes out the door.

"You just have to love her, Amelia," says Ellen.

"You're right. I guess I do," says Amelia.

Carlota

Carlota is dead. Zia received a letter from David that had been routed through Mexico. The postmark on the letter was October 13, 1961. Zia received the letter on December 14, two full months and a day later. The Cuban government had notified David of Carlota's death in Oriente. Officials in Oriente say she died of pneumonia. Doctors of the Rural Medical Service treated Carlota. These doctors with only stethoscopes, a few surgical instruments, and some basic medicines were not equipped to deal with Carlota's advanced pneumonia.

David was able to go to Oriente and retrieve her body. The guerrilla soldier Carlota loved was standing by her body when David arrived. The two did not speak. The guerrilla placed a Mariposa, a white ginger flower, on Carlota's body, bowed to David, and left.

David brought Carlota's body home to Miramar, to the house where Carlota grew up. As is the custom in Cuba, he had chosen a room in the house to display Carlota's body. After lining the room with chairs and setting out cups and thermoses of sweet black coffee, David was ready to receive mourners. Friends and neighbors, who kiss and hug tightly, came and stayed to tell stories of days long gone.

No one wore black.

Shocking everyone, Castro himself came to the wake. The socialist leader parted the crowd like Moses parted the Red Sea. A hush fell over the crowd. Castro hugged David like a long-lost brother before basically telling David that he, David, would have no control over Carlota's funeral. Castro insisted that Carlota's funeral be a secular one where Carlota's contribution to the Cuban government and its philosophy were to be touted.

Carlota was to be lauded for participating in the Literacy Movement, Castro told David. Castro agreed that Carlota's interment would be at the Colon Cemetery and had dictated that the funeral was to be held in Vedado for easy transport to the cemetery for burial.

All coffins in Cuba look alike. Coffins are covered in black cloth for adults and in white for children. There is a window for viewing the head of the deceased. Carlota's white-draped coffin is placed on a cart after the funeral and wheeled through the streets to the Colon Cemetery. A procession follows the coffin, and people line the street to watch the coffin go by.

Cubans lining the street play a game called tag. A Cuban lady touches her daughter and says, "Pasa el muerto." The daughter turns to the lady next to her, taps her arm, and says, "Pasa el muerto." The lady turns to the man next to her and says, "Pasa el muerto." The person at the end of the line who receives the last tap of the shoulder or pat on the arm cannot pass the phrase and knows he or she will be the next to die.

The state provides old black and yellow Russian taxis to carry the family to Colon Cemetery, but David refuses the taxi ride. Instead, he walks alongside Carlota's coffin. From time to time, David presses the palm of his hand on Carlota's coffin as if he can hold on to Carlota this way.

Colon Cemetery is home to hundreds, maybe thousands of souls—souls including La Milagrosa—The Miraculous Lady. La Milagrosa died in childbirth and was buried with her baby at her feet. When the grave was unearthed years later, La Milagrosa and her child were intact, but the baby was resting in the mother's arms, not near her feet.

Exhumation of graves is a common practice in Cuba. The poor are buried in pine boxes, which they later stack on shelves in a massive grave. The bodies remain in their boxes for two to three years until nothing is left but bones. The grave may be opened at that time, and the bones placed in a concrete box.

The boxes of bones are then labeled on the outside and stacked in the mausoleum. Someone in the family has to pay rent for the box to remain in the mausoleum. When the bones turn to ashes, family members may choose to remove the box and spread the ashes in a place with meaning for the deceased.

David's family, the Focas, have a family plot in the Colon Cemetery. He does not have to worry about Carlota's body being exhumed. With Carlota's passing, David has no family attachments left in Cuba. Just a few old friends and memories of happier times.

Her father is the one to call Ellen with the news of Carlota's death. He tells her Julio is devastated and is currently at Callander with Zia. The two mourn together. The family will hold a memorial service for Carlota at the Marshall Methodist Church on Christmas Eve Eve. Ellen will be there.

Carlota's death and talk of her funeral bring a flood of memories of her mother's death back to Ellen. It's traditional in the South for people to bring food to a family's home when they lose a loved one. Ellen remembers their living room, dining room, and kitchen flooded with people the night before her mother's funeral. The dining room table appeared to sag under the weight of the food brought to Ellen and her father by the townspeople.

Ellen vividly remembers helping Miss Mamie, flamboyant in her red floral dress, find a place for deviled eggs on the overcrowded dining table. Funny that Ellen remembers this detail. To this day, she can hear Miss Mamie gossiping with the Methodist ladies of the Esther Circle about the possibility of Ellen's mother committing suicide.

It was the night before the funeral when Ellen found out that Aunt Essie was moving from the Mitchell House in Marshall to Callander to live with Ellen and her father. Ellen did not like this idea initially, but Essie's moving in had saved Will and Ellen. Essie loved them, fed them, and helped them get on with their lives.

Ellen has a memory of Jo Jo standing outside their back door. Jo Jo came to console Ellen—so concerned for Ellen that he hadn't taken the time to change from his work clothes. Ellen tears up thinking about Jo Jo and his concern for her.

Ellen knows Zia, Julio, and especially David are feeling the deep, tearing pain she felt when her mother died. Ellen knows this pain lurks in the background of her life, even though three years have passed now. It may be there forever. Ellen bows her head and prays for them all.

A Letter from Jo Jo

The news of Carlota's death tilts Ellen's world. The world rights itself when she finds a letter from Jo Jo in the old university mailbox. Jo Jo always seems to level Ellen's world.

Dear Ellen,

I know you've been to Callander for Thanksgiving. I can see it all in my mind. Did you eat at the plantation house? Did Julio come? Did you see my mom and dad? I can never describe how much I miss it all. Bill and I ate hamburgers at the Mirage, a restaurant on base. Not exactly the turkey, dressing, gravy, green bean casserole, pecan pie Thanksgiving we're used to.

But I have to tell you; I'm loving living in Tripoli. You know, I always believed I'd travel far. Remember the poem I wrote for you:

I believe that I am an achiever and will travel far

No one believes that I will see
the world beyond Alabama

Being in Tripoli has taught me to appreciate a different culture. Besides the language, the Islam religion, and purdah — the interesting practice I told you about where the curtains separate the men from the women, just the feeling that I get here is so different. Remember how I loved Colorado? I love Libya, too. The feel of this place is a feeling of walking where the ancients walked. I read that archaeological finds indicate people inhabited Libya as far back as 10,000 BC.

Plus, just hearing about places like the Roman city of Leptis Magna and the ancient cave art at Tadrart Acacus add to this feeling of antiquity. My commanding officer is encouraging me to go to Tadrart Acacus, where I'll see a fantastic array of rock art. It's fascinating that the artwork reveals the development of man in this area in southern Libya. The earliest art shows animals, such as elephants, giraffes, hippos. Then humans appear, or human figures anyway, with round heads and no features, followed by drawings where humans are holding spears and having ceremonies. Next, horses and chariots appeared in the art, and finally camels appeared. I have to see this!

Now for the exciting news about Leptis Magna. Bill, Ilenia, and I went this past weekend, and I think I'll remember Leptis Magna forever. It's an ancient city on the Mediterranean and a two-hour drive east of Tripoli. The Phoenicians founded it in 1100 BC and lost it to Rome in 200 BC. You cannot imagine what it is like to walk into a Roman city and know that you are looking at a city that existed before Christ. And we were alone except for one elderly Italian man who collected money from us.

We walked into Leptis Magna under a massive arch built in honor of Septimius Severus, former emperor of Rome, and we followed a stone road to the baths. Amazingly enough, frescoes with vivid colors were on the bath walls showing scenes of hunting and, believe it or not, names of honored hunters. The murals could have been painted the day before. You can imagine noble Romans taking a communal bath in 200 BC.

Bill, Ilenia, and I walked Roman streets and saw foundations of small dwellings with irrigation systems. Pretty impressive for the time. I can't begin to describe the crumbling ornate columns, the temples, the forum, the market, and the statue, many of them headless. Of course, Bill and I did not have a clue what we were looking at. Ilenia explained it all.

The amphitheatre was my favorite. Ilenia said it could seat sixteen thousand people. Imagine circular rows of stone seating facing a circular walled arena. Behind the arena is a stone stage lined in the rear with tall columns—lintels for support still in place between the columns. Takes my breath away, just remembering it. Bill, Ilenia, and I sat at the top of the amphitheatre and could look beyond the stage and columns to see the Mediterranean with its beautiful shades of blue and dancing lights topping the waves.

I would love to sit at the top of the amphitheatre at Leptis Magna with you.

Love,

Jo Jo

Go to Ellen's Notebook at the end of the book to see pictures of Leptis Magna.

The Peabody Award Story

Ellen walks in the broadcasting studio to be confronted by Sandra. "Have you heard the news? Dr. Shelby is over the moon over Luke's Peabody entry. He's already claiming Luke is a winner."

Ellen is confused, and it's obvious. Sandra sneers at Ellen. She knows something about Luke that Ellen doesn't know and appears to take great pleasure in telling Ellen about it.

Ellen turns her back on Sandra and looks up at a monitor where Luke's story is airing to the broadcasting staff.

Kennedy, who inherited Eisenhower's plan to invade Cuba, was adamant the United States involvement in the Bay of Pigs not be revealed. Kennedy called off the second phase of the operation as the Brigade 2506 pilots were taxiing for takeoff. This action left Castro with combat aircraft. The very planes that Kennedy refused to destroy wreaked havoc on Brigade members. Approximately 80 percent of Castro's air force was disabled. The six planes not destroyed were the ones to combat the Brigade on the day of the Bay of Pigs invasion.

Another problem with the invasion was the location--the Bay of Pigs was Castro's favorite place to fish. The locals loved him. The largest swamp in Cuba surrounds the Bay of Pigs. Any other Cubans...

Dr. Shelby, pipe in one hand and lighter in the other, bustles up to Ellen. "Ellen, we have a winner here. Luke's story is phenomenal. I'm telling you something you already know. I'm sure you agree..."

"Dr. Shelby, I didn't know about Luke's story. He's kept it secret, even from me."

"The interviews, Ellen. That's what makes the story. Watch this..."

Ellen's attention turns back to the screen.

... two American Navy destroyers, the USS Eaton and the USS Murray. The ships tried to rescue more of the men in the water, but Cuban forces fired on the ships to prevent them from approaching for a rescue. This part of the story is from the American serviceman's perspective and what an amazing story he tells. His story starts with the USS Essex, which was on its way from Norfolk, Virginia, to the Caribbean to conduct ASW exercises...

Ellen's gut clenches. *No! It's Zia's! He's stealing Zia's story!*

Ellen looks across the studio. A large crowd of broadcasting students is watching the story as it concludes, and Luke tags the story. Luke is in the middle of the students who are crowding in to hug him, pound him on the back, congratulate him.

Ellen freezes, watching Luke accept congratulations for her Aunt Zia's story. Maybe sensing her, Luke turns to make eye contact with Ellen. Luke's expression of elation turns to fear. Ellen can see it in Luke's eyes. It's like watching happiness drain from a cup. Nothing left but the dregs of happiness and a frozen, dead expression with trembling lips.

Ellen turns and stumbles out of the broadcasting studio. She is trying to stop the biting taste at the back of her throat from erupting. The tears come, flowing down her face, clouding her vision.

"Ellen…"

Ellen knows Luke has come out of the J building and is following her. Ellen runs to her dorm room, where Luke can't follow. Where she can stay away from Luke and not have to see him again. This is the man she was to marry? A thief? Ellen throws herself across her bed, burrows her head in her pillow, and cries her heart out. All of Zia's work, duplicated by Luke, just so that he can win an award. Just so he can be a broadcaster in a major market.

Ellen thinks of Will and Amanda's wedding, where she told Luke she loved him for the first time. She thinks of the furniture taken from David Henry's attic to be in a home she would one day share with Luke. She thinks of the Bowl, where Luke covered her body with his. Ellen loved Luke. How could she be so wrong in the choice of someone to spend forever with?

Ellen thinks of Zia. She knows she has to call her. Zia has been hurt so badly—being imprisoned in La Cabaña, then forced to leave her husband behind in Cuba. How can Ellen begin to tell her this news about Luke? Then she remembers the Revolutionary War Soldier,

Jonas Stockman. *Truth and Honor.* Yes, Jonas is right, as always.

Ellen walks out in the hall to the wooden phone booth, sits on the worn seat, picks up the receiver, and dials the operator. Placing a direct call to Callander, she hears the operator ask Zia if she will accept charges on a call from Ellen Jones. Zia agrees.

"Ellen, so good to hear from you."

"Good to hear your voice, Aunt Zia. My heart breaks over Carlota. Are you still planning the memorial service on the night before Christmas Eve?"

"Yes. Julio will be home from school. So will you. It's the best time for the service."

"Any more word from Uncle David?"

"Nothing. I can't stand it, Ellen. You know how he's hurting—losing a child, being alone in a country that he once loved."

"I know he's hurting. I think he needs to be at Callander. That's what healed you after La Cabaña."

"I pray so hard every day for that miracle. I know God hears me."

"I know he does, Aunt Zia." A long pause. Ellen gathers her courage.

"Ellen, are you there?"

"Yes, ma'am. I have something bad to tell you." Pause. "I don't want to tell you."

"Whatever it is, as long as it doesn't concern David, I can handle it. Just tell me, Ellen."

"Luke stole your story."

"What?"

"I think I told you Dr. Shelby encouraged all of us to enter the Peabody competition. My story is about Mr. Chenard. Luke kept his story a secret. When I went to the broadcasting studio today, everyone was clamoring over Luke. His story was airing in the studio to the broadcasting students. Dr. Shelby was over the moon, declaring Luke a winner before the story was even submitted to the Peabody Awards committee. It was your story, Aunt Zia. The story told to you by the American serviceman and the member of the Brigade."

"You're positive?"

"Yes. Luke's story duplicates the American serviceman talking about the ghosting of his ship. He even tells about the role the USS Eaton played at the Bay of Pigs."

No sound from Zia. Ellen begins to cry.

Finally, Zia asks, "Did Luke reveal the names of the serviceman and the Brigade member I interviewed?"

"As far as I could tell, no. I didn't see the whole story, but I don't think Luke revealed their names."

"I can deal with this, as long as the interviewees are protected. You have to deal with it, too. Does Dr. Shelby know?"

"Oh no, he thinks Luke is a Peabody winner, for sure."

"We have to tell him, Ellen. I know you. You think you must tell Dr. Shelby, but it's my story. My duty to call Dr. Shelby."

"What do you think will happen?"

"Luke will not be submitting my story to the Peabody Award

committee. I can assure you he will not. As for any action Dr. Shelby takes, I can only guess. Best not do that now, Ellen."

"I'm sure Dr. Shelby is still at the broadcasting studio. You have the number?"

"Yes, all of us have it in case we need to contact you there."

"Will you call me after you've talked to Dr. Shelby?"

"You know I will. And Ellen, you don't realize it yet... or maybe you do. I think you're losing as much as any of us in this sad tale."

"I love you, Aunt Zia."

"Truth and honor, Ellen. I love you, too."

A Cuban Party

Mr. Chenard sends a taxi to Ellen's dorm to collect her on Sunday, the night of the Cuban party. The cab delivers her to a house on Calle Ocho, where Mr. Chenard is standing out front, waiting for Ellen. It's a yellow stucco house. Lime-green metal awnings hang over the front door and windows. The house is a bright yellow box with green trimmings, like the perfect package. Ellen barely has time to take it in before Mr. Chenard opens the taxi door to welcome her.

"Welcome to Calle Ocho! You are part of Little Havana now."

"Thank you. Mr. Chenard. And you're looking handsome tonight in what looks like a new guayabera. Am I right?"

"Yes, young lady. Purchased in your honor, of course. But we are wasting time. Come in. Come in."

Mr. Chenard holds the front door open, and Ellen steps into a world of color, sounds, and smells unlike anything she's experienced before. The scents of half-smoked cigars, rum, and sweat blend in the thick air. Cigars are smoked by both men and the women. Open bottles of rum are lined up at the back of each of the tables, lining the walls, and sweat drips from dancers moving in the middle of the room.

Mr. Chenard explains to Ellen that they are dancing the mambo, a dance of freedom in which dancers feel the music and express themselves to its rhythmic beat. The music pours into the room from a chunky radio set on one of the tables. The station is playing Cuban music, mambo from Perez Prado. The music changes and a slower song begins to play. The dancers dance the romantic danzón.

"Oh, Ellen. This party takes me back to Cuba. On Sunday afternoons, we listened to Radio Progreso, where artists performed live on-air. I remember dancing the danzón with my Louisa." Mr. Chenard hums and holds a pretend Louisa in his arms as he slowly dances.

Ellen turns from Mr. Chenard's dance and notices for the first time the children running around the adults, shouting and laughing and in their own world. There are old men playing dominoes in the next room. Their open collars reveal tan chests with tufts of wispy gray hair. They clamp cigars between their teeth. Rivulets of old age ripple out across their faces. Ellen can hear the clinking sound the dominoes make as the men place their tiles on the tables. A shout from one of the men as he places a double tile jolts her.

Mr. Chenard stops his dance when he sees Ellen's attention is fixed on the domino players. "All over Cuba, the people play dominoes. In Havana, it was not unusual to see players on sidewalks, front porches, and in parks. Four people play, with two partners playing against the other two partners. We will have a game sometime."

Mr. Chenard steers Ellen to tables of food and introduces her to ladies arranging food on the tables. "Ellen, meet Bonita, Charo, and Diego, the best cooks on Calle Ocho."

Bonita, pretty in her full skirt and off-the-shoulder blouse, asks, "This is the young lady who is writing your story?"

"Yes. Ellen is a broadcasting student at the University of Columbus. She will be famous one day. You will see her on the television."

"Ooooh! So exciting to meet you, Ellen," says the woman Mr. Chenard introduced as Charo. Charo appears old enough to be Bonita's mother. Her deeply lined face and gray hair are slicked back from her face, forming a small bun at the back of her neck.

Diego, about Bonita's age, motions to her. "Here, Ellen. Eat with us," she says.

Ellen surveys the different types of dishes on the table in front of her and says to Diego, "Can you explain these dishes to me? They all look delicious."

"Claro. Of course." Picking up a dish, she says, "These are bocaditos—ham on sweet rolls." Pointing to another bowl, Diego adds, "And these are chiviricos. They're like a sweet wonton."

"And you must try the empanadas. They're made of ground beef, chicken, or ham. They're my specialty," says Charo.

"I want to try one of each," says Ellen. "And these little balls?"

"They're croquetas, made of ham. Delicious."

"Oh, I want some of those, too."

Mr. Chenard laughs at Ellen's enthusiasm. "Don't forget the drinks, Ellen. No rum for you tonight, but we can offer iron beer. It is a Cuban soft drink. And here you have a pineapple soda. And, of course, your American sodas."

"It all sounds delicious. I'll have the pineapple soda."

With her plate piled high with food, Ellen follows Mr. Chenard around the room as he introduces her to his friends. They find two chairs against the wall in the front room and settle in to eat.

"What is that music, Mr. Chenard?"

"Oh, that's Celia, our most famous singer. She's with the La Sonora Matancera band. She's made quite a name for herself. You know, she is American now. Last year, Celia left Cuba to perform with the band in Mexico, but Celia and her husband did not return to Cuba. Like so many of us, she left the land she loved—all because of Castro.

Ellen and Mr. Chenard sit quietly, listening to Celia as they enjoy the feast. When they finish eating, Mr. Chenard stands up, places his empty plate on the chair. He turns toward Ellen. "Now, young lady. You must do an old man the honor of a dance."

Diego, overhearing Mr. Chenard, takes her plate. "Yes, Ellen, you must dance with the old man."

"But I don't know how."

Bonita, walking up to the threesome, hears Ellen. "Chica, you can do this. Follow me. We're working with a four-four count. Put your two feet together. Do nothing on count one. On count two, slide your left foot forward. On count three, place the weight on your right foot. On count four, bring your left foot back to the right and shift weight to the left foot. See?"

"Okay. Maybe I can do that."

"Let's stand side by side, and you follow me." Bonita hums as she dances alongside Ellen. "Bueno. You've got it, chica! Now, we've just performed the man's part. For your part, you go back when the man goes forward. Come on. I'm the man. Let's dance. You'll see."

Bonita starts singing "Mambo No. Five" as she and Ellen perform the basic steps. "Okay, Juan David. Ellen is ready to dance the mambo."

"Juan David?" asks Ellen.

"My given name. You, Ellen, may call me Juan David. Or you can keep calling me Mr. Chenard. Whatever makes you comfortable. Now, I hear Las Hermanas Montoya. They're singing 'Mucho, Mucho, Mucho.' Let us see how we do."

Haltingly at first, smoother later on, Ellen and Mr. Chenard dance the mambo. The dancers sense something special is happening, and they clear the floor for Ellen and Mr. Chenard. Ellen forgets everything— Luke's betrayal, Carlota's funeral, even her Peabody story. She throws herself into the dance. She has never felt so creative. So free. She just wants to dance. When Las Hermanas sing the last note, the room is still. Then, roaring applause. These beautiful people who lost their country and found a new country in Miami are applauding for Ellen. Ellen begins to cry.

"Hey! None of that. I will never mambo with you again if that is your reaction," says Mr. Chenard.

"I think I've found something special. I love the mambo. You're a good partner, Mr. Chenard."

Mr. Chenard bows from the waist. "Thank you for dancing with an old man, and thank you for coming tonight. Now, I think we had better get you back to your dorm."

While Ellen says her goodbyes, Mr. Chenard hails a taxi from the busy street outside. When it stops, he insists on seeing Ellen back to her dorm. He wants to make sure she's safe. On the ride back to the party, after he has walked Ellen to her dorm and said his goodbyes, Mr. Chenard imagines what he might say to his Louisa, who seems so far away tonight. He misses her.

"Louisa, we have found a daughter!" he would tell her. He thinks about the long pause that would likely follow his excited pronouncement, then smiles. "Yes, Louisa." He speaks the words aloud. "I thought that is what you would say. Goodnight, my love. Goodnight."

Ellen Talks to Dr. Shelby

Ellen has not been to the J building since the day of Luke's betrayal. She knows she has to talk to Dr. Shelby before she leaves for the Christmas holidays. It's difficult to walk in the building with the awful memories of seeing Luke's story rolling on the studio televisions and meeting Luke's eyes across the room.

Just get it over with, Ellen. You know you've got to do this.

Ellen walks into an empty studio. All the other students have already left to go home for the holidays. Ellen is not discouraged. She knows she'll find Dr. Shelby in his office, holidays or no holidays.

"Well, there you are. I wondered if I'd see you before you left for home," says Dr. Shelby, taking his pipe from his mouth.

"I had to come. Did you talk to my Aunt Zia?"

"Yes, Ellen. She called the day we aired Luke's story here in the studio. I tell you, my heart is sore. I've never been more wrong about a student. I would have sworn on a stack of Bibles that Luke would never be anything but honorable in his craft."

"I know, Dr. Shelby. But he was not honorable. Aunt Zia had talked to me about the content of the interviews she conducted. I recognized immediately that Luke's story replicated what Aunt Zia told me."

"Yes, your Aunt Zia confirmed this when I read Luke's script to her. Her main concern was for the interviewees."

"Please tell me Luke didn't reveal their names."

"No, Ellen. He had enough honor to keep the names protected."

Ellen thinks of Jonas Stockman. *Truth and honor.* She can't think of honor and Luke at the same time.

"Do you know what will happen to Luke? Will he be expelled?"

"No decision has been made at this time, but I would be surprised if Luke can stay and graduate. It's the university's decision. More precisely, the Board on Academic Honesty makes the decision. The Board can expel Luke for violating the Standards of Student Conduct."

"Do you think the Peabody is that important?" asks Ellen.

"It would probably guarantee placement in a major market."

"Oh, yes. Luke made it clear he wanted to be in a major market. He wanted to *start* in a major market. Not easy to do." Ellen can't keep the sarcasm from her voice.

"He'll be lucky to get a job in any market now," says Dr. Shelby. "What a waste. It breaks my heart."

"It breaks my heart, too." Stillness. Dr. Shelby and Ellen think of the larger-than-life Luke and how he seems to fill any space he was in. So hard to think of him gone from the university and the broadcast journalism department.

"I'm on my way home now," says Ellen. "My flight leaves in an hour. I guess I better get out to the airport."

Dr. Shelby stands and pats Ellen on the shoulder. "Go on, Ellen. Go to your Callander, and have a wonderful healing time with that wonderful family of yours. And please give my regard to your father, to Amanda, and especially to the indomitable Zia."

Ellen leans over and hugs Dr. Shelby. "You leave this studio. Don't stay here another minute. Go enjoy the season!" she says to him.

"Yes, ma'am." Dr. Shelby smiles as he watches Ellen straighten her shoulders and head out of the studio. *What a girl! I'll bet my last dollar it's Ellen we'll see in a major market after graduation.*

Ellen is walking under the low-hanging branches of the old oak trees, heading to her car, when she senses Luke. Strange, she does sense him. Looking up, Ellen sees Luke with his parents. Their car is parked at the curb up ahead. Luke's father is placing a suitcase in the trunk of a new Chevrolet. Luke and his mom are just standing there, watching. Do Luke's parents know? How will they stand it when they do? Ellen guesses that Luke is only going home for Christmas and will be back to face his sentence after the new year.

Ellen doesn't want Luke and his family to see her, so she stands very still until they get in the car and drive away. Then she begins to walk toward her dorm. Only in the periphery of her mind is Ellen beginning to understand that she could never marry Luke. She had been right to question where her career would fall in the scheme of things. It seems Luke would have done anything to get to the top. The world for Ellen is falling apart—a massive part of her world, anyway. Gone are the marriage plans. No saying, "I do" on the porch at Callander. No honeymoon. No sharing the life ahead of them.

Amelia and her family are in New York City, and she has lent Ellen her car to drive to the airport. It's a '56 Ford. A far cry from the brand new Chevy Luke drove away in. Her bags are already piled in the back of the Ford, and she's on her way to the airport. Ellen is crying, huge gulps of crying, sobbing almost. Ugly sounds are coming from her as she makes her way to the airport for her journey back to Callander. Her heart is hurting so badly.

Arriving at the airport, Ellen parks in long-term parking. She takes a shuttle to the terminal. Fellow travelers notice her swollen face and look away, in too much of a hurry to get involved.

Once aboard the plane, Ellen takes her seat next to a lady who could be a grandmother. Ellen thinks this because of the woman's wrinkled but kind face. "Are you all right, young lady?" she asks Ellen.

Ellen is silent until it hits her. She has Callander and all its people waiting ahead at the end of this flight. Ellen turns to the kind lady. "Yes, ma'am. I'm fine. I'm going to be fine."

Christmas in Alabama

Ellen is riding through Marshall in her father's car. He has picked her up and they are on their way to Callander. Spotting the Dairy Queen, Ellen laughs as she remembers all the times she drove around the Dairy Queen with Liz, looking for boys. There was a huge pothole behind the Queen. Ellen and Liz would drive around, hit the pothole, bounce to the ceiling of the car, and laugh uproariously. Not much luck finding boys, but very fun times.

Liz was Ellen's best friend from elementary school right through their senior year at Marshall High School. Come to think of it, Liz is still her best friend. Liz attends Marshall College, where Ellen's mother attended and later worked. Liz wants to teach high school English. Ellen thinks she's a brave soul for teaching at the high school level. All the angst!

Come to think of it, Ellen decides Liz is just the medicine she needs to deal with what has happened with Luke and the hurt she's living. She'll make that happen. But first, family time. Before Will completely stops the car, Ellen opens the door, steps onto the running board outside the car door, and races into Zia's arms.

Ellen can't help it. The tears start. She tries so hard to hold them back, not wanting her father to see how upset she is. The harder she tries, the less control she has.

"Hey, Ellen girl. Nothing can be that bad," says Will. Ellen looks at Will over Zia's shoulder and understands now that Zia has left the telling of Luke's story to Ellen.

"Come in, Ellen," her father says, wrapping his arm around her waist. "We'll have some coffee and some of Amanda's coffee cake and get to the bottom of this."

Ellen follows her father and Zia into the familiar kitchen. Will notices that Ellen is looking around. He says, "Amanda is away in town. It's just us. What's wrong?"

Ellen starts at the beginning, back in Miami when Zia invited Luke to accompany her on her interviews with the Brigade 2506 member and the American serviceman. She relays to her father how Aunt Zia had told Ellen about the content of the interviews later, during her visit at Thanksgiving. That's how Ellen had known that day when she walked into the J school to hear Luke's Peabody story airing in-house that Luke had stolen Zia's material.

No one speaks, but sounds fill the room and underscore their feeling—Ellen crying, Zia sipping her coffee, and fabric scratching against fabric as Will removed a handkerchief from his back pocket.

"You've broken with Luke?" asks Will.

"I haven't talked to him at all. Luke was in the studio when Dr. Shelby aired his story. He looked at me, and he saw that I knew it was Zia's story. I walked away. Well, ran is more like it."

"So, what has happened…?" asks Will.

Zia interrupts, "My story. My responsibility. I called Dr. Shelby immediately after Ellen called me. Dr. Shelby shared Luke's script with me. It's my story, all right."

"So, what happens to Luke?" asks Will.

"We'll find out after Christmas. Dr. Shelby thinks Luke will be expelled," Ellen says.

"I so regret this, Ellen. I must admit, I'm stunned. All of us at Callander liked Luke."

"I know, Dad. I did, too. We were going to marry, for gosh sakes."

"A lot of sadness, with this and Carlota's memorial service right around the corner. But this is Callander. We will always celebrate Christmas, no matter what's occurring in our worlds," says Will.

"Yes," says Zia. "David Henry is hosting his famous eggnog party tonight, so get your party shoes on. We're going to celebrate Callander and all those lucky enough to live on this land."

As she's done so very many times before, Ellen drives with her father, and now Amanda, to the plantation house for the nog party. And as always, Ellen gets a lump in her throat when she sees the plantation house adorned for Christmas with lit candles flaming in each window. An enormous live wreath hangs on the front door. It is a welcome sight, and she is happy to be back home for Christmas.

David Henry himself throws open the door as they walk up the steps to the porch of the old house. "There's my girl. Ellen! I've been waiting for you to make this party complete."

Standing on tiptoes, Ellen bear hugs her grandfather, holding on a little longer than usual. What this man means to her! David Henry taught Ellen about prejudice in the world by having her read and discuss books like *Uncle Tom's Cabin* by Harriet Beecher Stowe and *The Diary of a Young Girl* by Anne Frank. He talked to her about water fountains marked "Colored" and "White" and why this was wrong.

David Henry doesn't want his sharecroppers, black and white, exposed to the discrimination prevalent in Marshall and other towns nearby. The sharecroppers rarely leave Callander except for church. This is by their choice. They grow everything they need to eat. Or they buy it at the Callander commissary. If they need a doctor, David Henry brings the doctor to Callander. Ellen used to think David Henry sheltered the Callander people. Now she understands: he's protecting them.

David Henry is one of those men that other men respect. The workers on the plantation look up to him just as the men who come out to seek his advice on various matters in Marshall do. David Henry models for Ellen how to be a person of respect and how to respect others. She loves him so!

"So, you decided to come home from that university?"

"You can't keep me from Callander for long, Grandfather."

"That's good to hear." Turning to Will, David Henry says, "Will, I'm sorry. I ignored you and Amanda. So glad to see our girl home."

Will pumps David Henry's hand. "That's okay. I understand how you feel. It's wonderful to have her back."

"And Amanda. You grow more beautiful each day. Welcome to Callander."

"Thank you, David Henry. I understand I need to try some of the special eggnog."

David Henry laughs. "Oh, you fit right in here, Amanda. Come with me. I'll see that you get the right nog."

There's eggnog and there's eggnog with a kick at the plantation house Christmas party. It's a party for everyone living on plantation land, to include the sharecroppers and their children. Everyone knows that the nog on the left is for the women and children, and the nog on the right, spiked with Jim Beam, is for the men. Lila, David Henry's housekeeper, stands guard over the eggnog on the right, making sure no children get a sip of the potent nog.

Entering the grand hall that runs down the middle of the plantation home, Ellen spots the nine-foot Christmas tree, shining indeed with its shiny ornaments and bubble lights of red, green, and blue. In her mind's eye, she sees Jo Jo, just as she last saw him during Christmas, standing beyond the Christmas tree in his Air Force Academy uniform, so handsome he takes one's breath away. Jo Jo seems so real, but she knows it is just her imagination. Ellen starts to walk toward the place she imagines him standing when she feels a light touch on her arm. Turning, she sees Jo Jo's mother and father.

"Ellen, it's so good to see you," says Mrs. Reed.

"Mr. and Mrs. Reed, I was just thinking about Jo Jo."

Mrs. Reed smiles. "I think of him all the time, way over in Africa of all places."

Mr. Reed reaches around his wife to shake Ellen's hand. "Good to see you, Miss Ellen."

Ellen feels the rough calluses on Mr. Reed's hand as he shakes her own, calluses formed from working Callander land.

"So good to see you both." It's true. Ellen is glad to see Jo Jo's parents—the parents of the boy who kissed her in the grassy field at Callander, the boy who wrote a poem just for her. "Jo Jo and I write to each other. Did you know?"

"Oh, yes. Jo Jo tells us about his letters from you when he writes. What an adventure he's having!" says Mr. Reed.

"Yes, I try hard but admit I fail to see the land and people he's describing. My imagination lacks something, for sure. He's told us about the new and old cities, the desert, and his roommate. I understand you and Bill have something in common, right?" says Mrs. Reed.

"Yes, if you mean broadcasting. We do. I love hearing about the station and the programming over in Libya," says Ellen.

"I'm so glad you and Jo Jo stay in touch. It's so good to see you. We'll tell Jo Jo we saw you," says Mrs. Reed.

"And now, we'll pay our respects to Mr. Callander. Hope we see you again before you leave, Ellen" says Mr. Reed.

"I'll make sure you do," she says. It hits her all at once, as Mr. and Mrs. Reed walk away, that they made no mention of Ilenia. Ellen smiles. Being at Callander makes her heart happy. She heads for the eggnog table—the one for women and children, of course.

Ellen has made arrangements to meet Liz for lunch at the drugstore in Marshall. Entering the store, Ellen is surprised to see Bobby Jenkins still standing behind the soda fountain. Bobby is in the process of pulling down a shiny spigot to release soda into a glass.

"I'll have one of those, Bobby."

"Ellen Jones. So good to see you home. I'll be right with you. Let me finish this making this cherry soda for Liz."

Turning, Ellen spots Liz in one of the cherry-red booths that line the right side of the fountain area of the drugstore. Beautiful Liz with her dark hair full hanging below her shoulders and her knockout smile. Ellen remembers that Liz was Miss Marshall their senior year in high school.

"Well, hello there, Miss Marshall, Class of '59."

"Oh, Ellen." Liz slides out of the booth. She is hugging Ellen before Ellen can put her soda on the table.

Ignoring the soda that splashes out of the glass, Ellen hugs her right back. "Liz, girl. Don't you ever get ugly?"

Liz throws her head back and laughs.

"I'm so glad to be home, Liz."

Liz notices the seriousness behind her friend's statement.

"And I'm so glad you're here. Everything all right?"

Looking at Liz, Ellen decides it is all right. Everything is all right. She will deal with Luke when the time comes. Their relationship is over. There is no going back. Ellen doesn't want to rehash the whole thing with Liz. Enough! Ellen smiles at Liz.

"Tell me what's happening in Marshall. Still want to teach?"

"Yes, Ellen, more than ever. One more year at Marshall College, and I'll be able to teach."

"Any idea where?"

"You won't believe this, Ellen, but I'll be teaching English at Marshall High after graduation.

"No way!"

"Yes. Miss Taylor is retiring. I think the indomitable Miss Taylor is waiting for me to graduate so that I can take her place. As if I could ever do that."

Ellen brings the image of Miss Taylor to mind. Riotous red hair surrounds the teacher's face adorned with a pair of oversized purple-rimmed glasses. A huge smile usually spreads across the bottom part of Miss Taylor's face. Ellen loves her. Miss Taylor is the sponsor of *The Voice*, the school newspaper that Ellen edited her senior year in high school.

"Will you sponsor *The Voice* as well?"

"I think that's the plan."

"I envy you, Liz, with your life all laid out. Who knows where I'll land."

"Well, I envy you the excitement that will follow you and your career, not that I'm not happy right here in Marshall."

"Speaking of Marshall, what's the news?"

"Remember Mable? She's telling everyone that Jo Jo Reed is writing to her."

Ellen's stomach tightens. Her memories of Mable are not good ones. Mable was always in competition with Ellen over everything from the school play to trying to win Jo Jo's affection. To Ellen's knowledge, she never won Jo Jo. Or did she? Surely Jo Jo is writing to Mable to be kind. That's the way he is, after all.

"Aw, come on, Ellen. You know ole Mable will never get Jo Jo."

Ellen relaxes. Liz could always do that for her.

"And would you care if she did?"

Ellen senses this is a serious question deserving a serious answer.

"I think I do care, Liz. Mable is not good enough for Jo Jo."

"But you are. Advice, girlfriend. Don't get so infatuated with what's in Miami that you forget what's right here in Marshall."

"Oh, Liz. You always make me look at life a little differently. It's fabulous to be with you."

"And you, too, Ellen. I've got to run though. Have a meeting. I'll see you at the memorial service tonight." Reaching over the booth, Liz grabs Ellen in a tight hug.

Long after Liz leaves, Ellen remains in the cherry-red booth, thinking about home and pondering what the future may bring.

Carlota's Memorial Service

The old Methodist Church in Marshall was built in the 1840s "when cotton was king." Wealthy plantation owners built stately homes in town while they farmed hundreds of acres out of town. These wealthy plantation owners wanted a church of some significance to worship in on Sunday mornings, so the planters bought Marshall Methodist, an architectural wonder with multiple spires that reached heavenward

Impressive medieval-style windows arched at the top. Inside the church were marble floors and plastered walls and pews made of cherry wood. The Callander and Jones families have worshipped here for generations.

Essie and Ellen are in the narthex. Aunt Essie is in the middle of telling Ellen about William Clinton Jones and Martha Ruth Mitchell, Will and Essie's parents who were married in this sanctuary. Amanda has joined Essie and Ellen, and Will walks over to the three of them.

"Have you two heard from Zia? It's past time for the service to start, and she's not here."

Julio joins them. "I have the same question. Where's Zia?"

"I haven't seen her all day," adds Amanda.

"I'm beginning to worry. The service was to start ten minutes ago. Where can Zia be?"

"Have no anxiety about anything. Philippians 4:6," Essie quotes from memory.

"Well, we can't start the service without Zia. Should we go to the plantation house to look for her?" her father asks.

"I'll go," says Julio. "Funny. Mr. Callander is already seated in the sanctuary. You'd think if something were amiss, he would mention it."

Before Julio can leave the narthex, the heavy doors open, and Zia walks in. She's not alone. With her is a tall, slim man, well over six feet tall. Even though his black hair is tinged with gray and deep lines cut through his face, curving around his mouth, this man is handsome to the point of distinction. There is no mistaking who it is. It's David Foca.

"Papi," yells Julio. He runs to throw himself against his father.

Holding Julio to his chest, David openly begins to cry.

"Está aquí," says Julio. "I didn't know if I'd see you again."

David, chin on top of Julio's head, looks at Zia. "You didn't think I'd leave you and this beautiful lady forever, did you?"

Zia smiles back at David. "I know all of you have a thousand questions for David. I have a few myself, but I suggest we go into the sanctuary and honor Carlota. Do you think she'll mind a memorial service in a Methodist church?

"Yes, I do," says David, smiling back. "She's probably arguing with God at this very moment about the fact that we're not honoring her memory in a Catholic church."

Everyone in the narthex laughs, remembering how very argumentative Carlota could be. One by one, the family members line up to follow David and Zia into the sanctuary to honor Carlota's life in this church of the American south, so far removed from Cuba but much the same as they have gathered to observe the rituals surrounding death.

As the family enters the sanctuary, Miss Mamie, who represents the church's Esther Circle, hands each family member a copy of the program that Zia has designed for the memorial service. Remembering how Carlota loved Raphael, Zia has placed a copy of the Italian artist's *The Sistine Madonna* on the cover of the program.

As the last person enters the sanctuary and settles in a pew, Zia stands and walks to the altar. Glancing around the sanctuary, she makes eye contact with family members and friends, then begins to speak. "We are here to memorialize the passing of Carlota Foca," Zia says. "Born in 1944, Carlota was just seventeen when she died this October of pneumonia.

Carlota was serving in Castro's Literacy Brigade in Cuba when she passed. The Literacy Brigade is a program to bring literacy to all peoples of Cuba. Thousands of adults and schoolchildren like Carlota traveled to mostly rural areas to teach people to read. Carlota lived with various families, working alongside them in the fields during the day and teaching the families to read at night.

Carlota was in Oriente, Cuba, when she died. David brought her to Havana to bury her. While Carlota's funeral has already occurred in Havana, we gather here tonight to remember her life.

Carlota was an art lover, so I chose a work by Raphael, one of her favorite artists, to adorn the front of the memorial bulletin. Carlota's favorite Bible verse is in the program. Julio will come to share the verse with you now."

Julio solemnly walks to the front of the sanctuary as Zia sits down. Julio begins. "I'm so sorry that most of you did not know my sister. She was bright beyond her years. And so sure of herself. I think you could say she was a force." Julio smiles as he recognizes that most people in the congregation are smiling, too. "Her favorite Bible verse was Matthew 22: 37-39. Allow me to share this verse with you: 'Love the Lord your God with all your heart and with all your soul and with all your mind. This is the first and greatest commandment. And the second is like it: Love your neighbor as yourself.'"

Julio closes his Bible and walks back to the pew to sit down. Zia returns to the front of the sanctuary and faces the congregation.

"I had planned to tell you about Carlota, the person, but her father arrived from Cuba today and who better is qualified to talk about Carlota than him? David…" Zia motioned to her husband.

David stands and faces the congregation. He smiles before saying, "Carlota was born crying at the top of her lungs. The nurses said they'd never heard such loud crying from a newborn. And that's the way she faced life. Bold. Loud. Argumentative. But with a heart filled with love and deep devotion for her family and for the downtrodden. Carlota always wanted to save the oppressed. I think that's why Castro's Marxism appealed to her.

I can see her right after I married Zia. Zia, Carlota, and Julio traveled with me by train to the sugar cane plantations in Oriente. Carlota loved the land. She enjoyed talking with the workers. Oh, and she loved horses, too.

In my mind's eye, I see Zia, Carlota, and Julio racing on horses across the plantation land. Julio said she was a force…" David pauses and brings a tight fist to his mouth. Closing his eyes, he bites his fist as he cries uncontrollably.

Julio reaches David first. Taking David by the arm, Julio leads him back to his pew.

Moved, Zia faces the congregation. She thanks them again for coming. "We will close this service by singing the first verse of *'Silent Night, Holy Night.'*"

Julio stands with Zia and the voices rise from those who have gathered in the church. Ellen stands to sing with the congregation, but seeing David seated with head bowed and tears falling over clenched fists, she can't find her voice. Ellen prays instead as she listens to others sing.

Silent night, holy night!
All is calm, all is bright.
Round yon virgin, Mother and Child
Holy infant so tender and mild,
Sleep in heavenly peace,
Sleep in heavenly peace.

As the last note fades, Julio sings in a clear voice:

¡Noche silenciosa Santa noche!
Hijo de Dios, pura luz del amor.
Vigas radiantes de tu rostro santo
Con el alba de la gracia redentora.

Jesús Señor, en Tu nacimiento.
Jesús Señor, en Tu nacimiento.

As the last note hangs in the air, those who came to memorialize Carlota walk silently from the sanctuary.

After the service, the family gathers in the kitchen at the plantation house. They're eager to hear David's story. After helping themselves to coffee and Lila's homemade pecan pie, they settle in to listen to his tale. In his soft voice, surprising for a man of his size, David begins.

"Ellen, you remember Paco and Luisa?"

"I'll never forget them," says Ellen. "Paco and Luisa took me in when I went to Cuba to bring Aunt Zia out. If you remember," she says, turning to the group gathered. "Paco and Luisa Perez worked on a plantation near Santiago, a plantation that once belonged to David. Paco's brother, Manuel, took me from Montego Bay, where I had been vacationing with the broadcasting students from school, to Paco and Luisa's house. I stayed with them until David could bring Zia from Havana."

"And you brought Zia back to Montego Bay?" asks Liz.

"Yes, Manuel came back for us. Zia and I rode in his boat to Montego Bay without incident. Is that how you got out, Uncle David?"

"Yes. Exactly."

Zia is hearing of David's escape for the first time as she remembers the trip with Manuel. Zia can see David in Manuel's boat, tarp ready in case he needs to hide. Zia is clutching David's right hand. She is afraid to let go. Afraid he isn't real.

Ellen, too, remembers how terrified she was—terrified that they would be stopped and returned to Cuba. Ellen remembered how she had planned to say she was a member of the Literacy Brigade if caught. Thank heavens, it was an easy trip from Cuba back to Montego Bay.

Smiling at Ellen, David reaches over with his left hand and takes Ellen's hand. David has square hands with cropped nails, and Ellen can feel the calluses formed from his work on the sugar cane plantations.

"My trip was exactly like yours, Ellen, with one exception. I brought Paco and Luisa out of Cuba with me."

"You did?" says Ellen.

"I had to," says David. "We were lucky the first time they helped, when you and Zia were with them. I couldn't take a chance and leave them behind this time. Castro would execute them for helping me."

"But where are they?" asks Zia.

"Paco has relatives in Miami. He and Luisa are with them for now. David Henry, I hope it's all right; I promised them a home at Callander if they didn't want to live in Miami."

"You don't have to ask. Of course, it's all right. You know we grow sugar cane here. Maybe you can start something on Callander land, and Paco and Luisa can help if they come."

"It would be our honor. I know Paco and Luisa would love it."

Julio has sat silently through David's story. Now, he says, "Well, Papi, before they put you in the fields, we've got so much to show you. You've got to see the Callander land and meet all the folks who live here. You've got to come with me to MMI to see the college, too." Julio grins, "And I have a girl I want you to meet."

David smiles into Julio's eyes, feeling wonder at this tall son of his. How fortunate he and Zia were able to send Julio out of Cuba and away from Castro.

Zia looks at father and son, together at Callander. *A miracle!* David, Julio, and Zia—each of them had paid a terrible price to be here, but they were together now.

JANUARY 1962

Ellen Says Goodbye to Luke

Ellen is on the flight back to the university, and her thoughts are of Luke. How strange! A future Ellen thought settled no longer exists. She is having a hard time adjusting to the idea. *No wedding. No shared careers. No Luke in her life.*

Ellen knows she'll have to deal with Luke. She's sure she'll see him before he leaves campus. That's assuming he will leave school. Ellen cringes at the thought of talking to him.

Once she's on campus, Ellen goes straight to the J building to see Dr. Shelby. Again, she finds him in his office.

"Did you go home at all for the holidays?" asks Ellen.

Dr. Shelby takes his pipe out of his mouth and smiles. "Yes, I did, young lady." The smile fades as he tells Ellen he came back to campus one day early for Luke's hearing with the Board on Academic Honesty.

"The board has made a decision?"

"Yes, and it's as we expected. Luke is expelled. His records will be marked as such."

"He's one semester away from a degree. I can't get over the waste. He's not a terrible person, Dr. Shelby. I'll never understand how he could steal Aunt Zia's story and feel he wouldn't get caught."

"He lost his way, Ellen. I hope he finds it again."

"Me, too," answers Ellen, realizing for the first time it's true. She does hope Luke recovers from his mistake and the consequences that have naturally followed.

Back in the dorm, Ellen goes through the motions, unpacking her suitcase and looking over next semester's schedule. She's not surprised when she hears the phone ring on her hall and someone yells, "Phone for Ellen Jones."

Dreading what's coming, Ellen picks up the phone. "Hello."

"Cotton, it's Luke. Can you meet me at the Bowl?"

"I don't think so, Luke. Too many memories. I'll meet you in front of my dorm."

Ellen takes her time walking down the steps to the first floor of Caldwell Hall and out the double doors. Luke is pacing in front of the dorm. He is the same gorgeous man with blue eyes, a square jaw, and dark hair that coils along his neck.

"Hello, Cotton," he says, looking into her eyes. She wonders what he's thinking now.

"Hello, Luke," Ellen whispers.

"You know I'm leaving Columbus. I've been expelled. I knew I'd be expelled before I left campus for the holidays."

Looking at Luke, the pain Ellen feels is almost physical. "Why did this happen, Luke? A job was more important than honor? Than a life with me?" Ellen overlaps her arms around her body. Pain.

"Anything you could say to me, I've already said to myself. I'm hurting, Ellen. I wish I could take it back, but it doesn't work that way." Luke hangs his head and stays that way for a long time, just looking down at the cold ground. Ellen doesn't move. Finally, he looks up again. "I love you, Ellen. I'll always love you."

Ellen cries. The tears she's tried to hold back come anyway. Ellen can't talk for the longest time. Can't answer Luke. Finally, Ellen stands straighter and looks at Luke. "I can't love you anymore, Luke."

Nothing else comes. There is no more to say. No, "What were you thinking?" No, "I hate what you did."

"I'm so sorry, Ellen. I screwed up so badly."

"I do care what happens to you, Luke. What will you do?"

"Mother has gotten me a job at the *Atlanta Journal*. I'm lucky. I'll be writing hard news stories. I'll work there until I can find a college or university that will allow me to transfer and finish my degree."

"I wish you luck, Luke. That's the best I can do right now."

"You know the very worst of it, Ellen? I've lost something more important than the Peabody Award."

Ellen knows that Luke means their relationship, the marriage they had both wanted. But she has nothing to say. She's empty.

Ellen turns and walks back into Caldwell Hall.

Every day, Ellen is reminded of Luke. All the places they were together—the movie theater, the Tea Room where students hang out, and, most of all, the J building. Only with her mother's supposed suicide has Ellen felt this raw before. The truth has peeled away her outer layer and left her feeling vulnerable, exposed.

A Letter from Jo Jo

On her daily trip to the campus post office, Ellen squats to peer through the little window on the front of her mailbox. Today, she sees blue—an indicator of an Air Force envelope and Jo Jo's letter inside. Turning the combination lock on the mailbox, she opens the small door and retrieves the letter.

As is her custom, Ellen sits on one of the benches outside the post office and opens Jo Jo's letter

Dear Ellen,

I have big news! I'll be leaving Tripoli this summer and will be home on leave for thirty days. Is that perfect? Hopefully, you'll be home for the summer and not off reporting on some news story. I'd love to spend some time with you before you go back to Columbus for your senior year.

Speaking of your senior year, do you know what you want to do after graduation? Have you nailed down what part of broadcasting you want to pursue? Directing, reporting, editing? Or, are you getting married?

I think I know you well enough to know marriage won't keep you from a career. Am I right?

I've more big news! Bill and Ilenia are engaged and will marry in Tripoli and return stateside this summer. I'd love for you to meet them. They made my stay in Tripoli, and you and Bill have broadcasting in common. You never know, maybe it'll happen.

Well, I'm going for now, lovely girl.

You know you'll always be my girl. Do you still have the poem I wrote for you? I hope you'll read it from time to time.

Love,

Jo Jo

Ellen puts the letter down and, realizing she's been holding her breath, lets go with a whoosh. Jo Jo does not love Ilenia; Bill does. Ellen knows herself well enough to know that she cares very much that Jo Jo doesn't love Ilenia.

She heads back to the dorm room. When she's inside her room, she reaches down to pull open the desk drawer, and takes out Jo Jo's poem. She reads the words she knows well.

I've lived so long on Callander land
that I know every inch by smell, taste, touch

I know I could leave if you went with me

My friends say that you'll never look at me

I believe that we could live together forever—anywhere

The combination of Jo Jo's letter from Tripoli and the old poem brings warmth. Ellen was left cold over Luke's actions and the sudden end to their relationship. Nice to feel this warmth in her life at this moment, when she needs it most.

Old Luella. Ellen remembers the stooped soothsayer with the long, curled fingernails and wispy gray hair. She recalls how the children of Marshall are so terrified of Luella that they cross the sidewalk to avoid walking near her. Ellen feels differently about Luella. She feels respect for the fortune-teller. After all, Luella made three predictions about Ellen's life at the time of Ellen's birth, and they all came true.

Ellen remembers one of Luella's three predictions: *You will find the soldier.* She had found Jonas Stockman. But is the soldier really Jo Jo? Ellen doesn't know. But Luella does.

This is Ellen Jones Reporting

Ellen walks into the broadcasting studio to find students gathered around a monitor. They are watching her Peabody Award entry about Juan David Chenard. Ellen smiles to see her friend, Mr. Chenard—he'll always be Mr. Chenard to Ellen—talk about his tenure at the University of Havana.

One of the broadcasting students sees Ellen. "Ellen, Dr. Shelby is over the moon about your story. He says it's a Peabody winner, for sure."

Ellen is touched to see some of her fellow broadcasting students crying over Mr. Chenard's story. It's a sad story, but a beautiful one. Ellen feels gratitude for Mr. Chenard and his lovely Louisa for allowing her to share their story

Dr. Shelby, pipe in one hand and lighter in the other, bustles up to Ellen. "Ellen, we have a winner here. Your story is phenomenal. I'm telling you something you already know. I'm sure you agree…"

Dr. Shelby pauses to look at the monitor as Ellen tags Mr. Chenard's story.

"This is Ellen Jones Reporting for Miami News Now."

Ellen's Notebook

Ellen loves Luke

70 sheets/college ruled
11x8½in/27.9x21.5cm

notebook

1961

LIGHTING

Chapter Two Notes

Lighting Categories

- Two categories of lighting are directional and diffused.

- Directional lighting is focused; it's a beam of light.

- Diffused lighting spreads out and covers a broader area.

Lighting in the Field

Reporters on location—or you can say reporters in the field—are lit using a triangular lighting plan consisting of key, back, and fill lights. Not to be misleading, the triangular lighting plan is used in the studio as well.

The key light is the primary source of light. Position the key light at a forty-five-degree angle to the left or right and above the subject. You may use a portable light, the sun, or another bright lighting in the environment for your key light. Key lights are usually directional but don't have to be if you want softer shadows.

The fill light fills in shadows caused by the key light. Position a portable light at a forty-five-degree angle on the opposite side of the key light. If no portable light is available, you may use a reflector.

A professional reflector is covered with reflective material and is used to bounce light to fill in shadows. If no professional reflector is available, use a white poster board. Fill lighting is diffused.

The backlight separates the reporter from the background. Position the backlight directly behind the reporter.

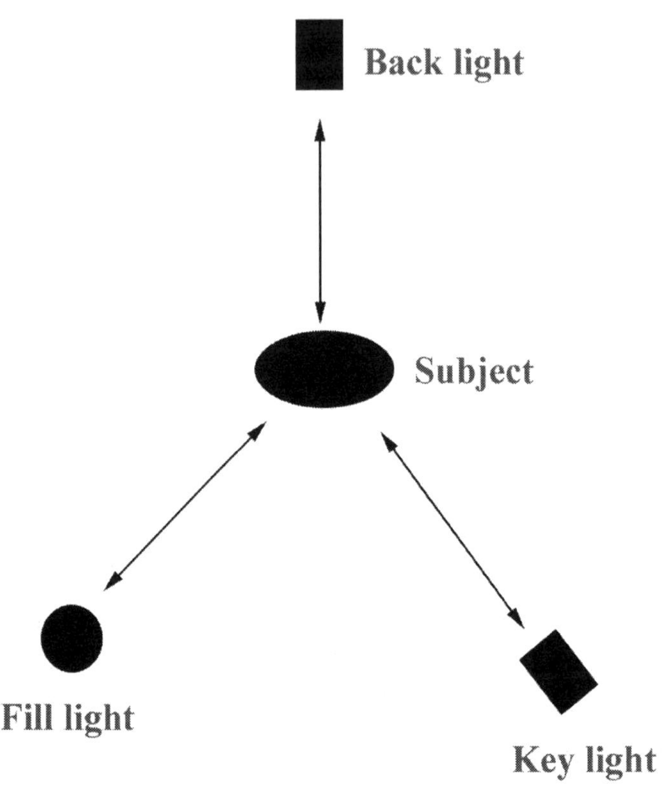

HARD NEWS STORY FORMS

Chapter Seven Notes

Readers

A Reader is a news story in which the reporter is seen throughout the story. A graphic may appear over the shoulder, but no footage is included. Readers are usually less than thirty seconds long.

Voiceover or VO

In a Voiceover, the viewer sees footage related to the story while the reporter narrates. The reporter is not seen on screen.

VO/SOT

SOT stands for sound on tape. This usually refers to a portion of an interview used to inform or support information in the story. In a VO/SOT, the viewer sees footage related to the story while the reporter narrates. The voiceover is followed by a SOT or portion of an interview. The SOT will, in most cases, be followed by more voiceover.

Donuts

An anchor or reporter starts a live delivery of a story, which is followed by film with the same person's voice narrating, followed by the anchor or reporter again appearing live.

Package

A Package or PKG is a complete story, with both audio and video elements edited on film. An anchor will introduce the package that rolls during the newscast.

EDITING RULES

Chapter Seven Notes

Cut on Motion

Cutting on motion keeps the viewer from noticing the edit. For example, the subject turns or looks down as the cut is made.

B-Roll

B-roll is additional footage used to illustrate and support the principal footage that tells the main story. For example, the principal footage consists of the reporter delivering the news, while B-roll shows a visual of what the reporter is saying. B-roll footage has to be significant to the story.

Constantly Change What the Viewer Sees

Don't let any shot last over two or three seconds, unless there is sufficient action in the shot to hold the viewer's attention. This holds true for B-roll footage as well.

Avoid Jump Cuts

Jump cuts occur when you cut from a shot of one person to another shot of the same person in the same scene, but the person's body has moved or something in the scene has changed. For example, shot one shows the reporter looking down, and shot two shows the reporter looking straight into the lens. There's no action to show how the reporter moved from looking down to looking into the lens. It's abrupt and jarring, which is why jump cuts should be avoided.

Jump cuts frequently occur when editing an interview. The editor shows one part of the interview and, cutting out a portion, moves to another part of the interview. Jump cuts can be repaired by inserting a close-up between the two shots. The close-up should relate to the action conveyed in the story.

Screen Direction

Avoid changing screen direction in a sequence.

If a subject is moving from left to right in one shot, he must not move from right to left in the next shot.

JO JO'S LETTER

Chapter Ten Notes

Riding into Tripoli from the base, you pass the harbor. The Red Castle is in the background. The Red Castle was initially built to defend the city. It is now a museum.

In the Old City, the Arch of Marcus Aurelius is the last existing remnant of the ancient city of Oea. The arch was built in AD 165.

The entrance to the ancient walled city.

This is an octagonal minaret in the old city. The muezzin, a servant of the mosque in good standing who has a strong voice, calls Muslims to prayer from atop the minaret.

You can't tell from this black and white photo, but the dome of the palace is gold. King Idris became king in 1951 and was the first king of Libya.

Inside the market in the old city.

JO JO'S LETTER

Chapter Fifteen Notes

Arab women are covered from head to toe in something called a barracan, a white wool garment that covers everything on their bodies with the exception of their right eye and their feet.

Men may wear barracans, too. The barracans men wear drape over the head and shoulders and hang near the knee.

MR. CHENARD

Chapter Sixteen Notes

This is La Catedral de la Virgen María de la Concepción, where David, Zia, and their two children attended church. La Catedral was built in 1777 and is also known as the Havana Cathedral. Interesting fact: the ashes of Christopher Columbus were kept in the cathedral in Old Havana from 1796 to 1898.

Inside La Catedral.

Old Havana has existed since the 1500s and encompasses the downtown area of Havana, Cuba's largest city by far. More pictures of Old Havana follow.

All over Cuba, the people play dominoes. In Havana, it is not unusual to see players on out on the street. Four people play, with two partners playing against the other two partners. It's a noisy game.

Opening in December 1930, this hotel was built for American tourists. At first, no Cubans were allowed to stay in the Hotel Nacional. Now a national monument, it is a source of pride for Cubans.

Mr. Chenard's University of Havana with its magnificent steps. Fidel Castro studied law here in the 1940s.

The Grand Theatre of Havana is an opera house and performing arts center. It houses the National Ballet of Cuba. Zia and David attended the opera here. It's in Old Havana as well.

JO JO AND ILENIA

Chapter Twenty-Three Notes

This is the luxurious Uaddan. I think most of Jo Jo's entertainment comes from movies on base, then dining and dancing the night away at the Uaddan on weekends.

A LETTER FROM JO JO

Chapter Thirty Notes

Leptis Magna was second only to Carthage as the most important city in Roman North Africa. Septimius Severus was born in Leptis Magna and later ensured that the city was home to many magnificent structures. The arch built in Severus' honor sits at the most important crossing in the center of the ancient Roman city.

Medusa was a beautiful mortal from Greek mythology. As legend has it, Medusa was turned into a vicious monster with snakes for hair by Athena, goddess of wisdom. Gigantic heads of Medusa decorate the new forum. Their purpose is to prevent bad luck.

In 1866, the French consul in Tripoli transported twenty-nine columns from Leptis Magna to France to be used in the building of Versailles.

Gladiators performed in the amphitheatre at Leptis Magna.

Acknowledgments

First, I want to thank my husband, L.C. Smith, who has supported me throughout my journey as a published author. Typical of L.C., he designed T-shirts featuring the cover of my first book, *Ellen and the Three Predictions*, to share with family and friends who wore them at book festivals in the area. It would be difficult to name all the ways he has supported me, so a huge thank you to my husband.

Cuba, during the late 1950s and early 1960s, plays a role in my young adult novels. So many people have helped me in my journey of discovery about Cuba. My Aunt Zena married a sugar cane plantation owner during Batista's reign, and she lived in Cuba. Aunt Zena sparked the idea of Cuba's role in my books. Other contributors are Mary Flynt, Evita and Heidi Hernandez, and our children, Doug and Christy Smith.

Mary Flynt was one of the Pedro Pan children who left her parents in Cuba and came to Miami. Mary has been invaluable to me as a source of information, not only about the Pedro Pan Movement but also about daily life in Havana after Castro rose to power.

Thank you to Evita and Heidi Hernandez for sharing their knowledge of Cuba with me over an Italian dinner. Both mother and daughter were in Cuba in 2018. They were invaluable in describing the sites of Havana, Cuban customs, and all the fabulous food and drink featured in Chapter Thirty-Four of this book.

Our children, Doug and Christy Smith, journeyed to Cuba in 2018 with Evita Hernandez, and they brought Havana alive for me with their photos and beautiful stories of the Cuban people.

A special thank you to our almost-lifelong friend, Senior Chief Petty Officer James R. McLendon, who is retired now after twenty-one years of active duty in the Navy. L.C. and I were friends with Jim for over forty years before discovering Jim was at the Bay of Pigs invasion. We were amazed to find out that his duty station was next to the commanding officer of the USS Eaton during the invasion. He was an eighteen-year-old Signalman Seaman at the time. Service members rarely share their stories, and I am humbled that Jim did.

Mimi Schroeder of Max Communications is my adventurous, highflying publicist. She has made a tremendous difference in how the Ellen books are presented to the world. Thank you, Mimi, for all you've done so superbly.

How do I begin to thank Dawn Richerson for her involvement in the editing and publishing of *This Is Ellen Jones Reporting?* Dawn is indispensable! My work is so much improved because of her. Dawn has been involved in all three of my books, and I consider myself blessed to work with her.

Donna Hill, Connie Corley, and Mary Grace Holder were beta readers of *This Is Ellen Jones Reporting.* What a difference they made in the telling of the story. Many thanks to all of them for their input and support.

It was great to rekindle a friendship with Judy Dixon who was in Tripoli when we were there. Thank you, Judy, for the photograph of the Uaddan.

Thank you to all my beautiful friends, including the Marys and the Amelia Island Girls, who supported me in ways that still leave me stunned. I can't name all of you for fear of leaving someone out, and I couldn't bear to do that. You know who you are—hugs and love to you.

I can't tell you how many times I've reached out to my wonderful children, Jeff and Katie, for technical support. Thank you for your patience, children.

I am so blessed to be a member of this particular Smith family— L.C., Jeff, Katie, Doug, and Christy. Those who know them agree that they are an amazing bunch of bright, creative, talented people who love life. They are fun!

About the Author

Alayne Smith is a retired broadcast journalism teacher who earned M. Ed. and Ed. S. degrees in Instructional Technology from the University of Georgia. She taught broadcast journalism for fifteen years in Gwinnett County, Ga., where she developed the very first broadcast journalism course at the high school level.

With other Gwinnett County broadcast journalism teachers, she contributed to the development of an eight-course continuum of courses in broadcast journalism and video production. Two of Alayne's students won the 1999 Southern Regional Student Emmy Award from the National Academy of Arts and Sciences. Sixty of her students produced documentaries and feature stories, advancing to International Media Festivals held in New Orleans, Dallas, Houston, Indianapolis, and Denver. Alayne served as a committee member for the International Student Media Festival from 1995 to 1998 and as a CNN Student Bureau Advisor from 1999 to 2001.

While working at the Broadcast and Learning Department of Gwinnett County Public Schools, Alayne created classes, developed manuals, and designed a cluster training approach for media specialists in grades K through 8 to maximize the use of each school's broadcasting equipment. She co-taught sessions in each of the county's seventeen clusters, reaching media specialists from over ninety-six schools. Media Specialists were offered hands-on instruction to assist them with creating informative, curricula-based, and attention-getting broadcasts.

Ellen and the Three Predictions, published in March 2017 by Cactus Moon Publications, is Alayne's first novel. The historical fiction novel written for young adults is set in the late 1950s and early 1960s and details the life of aspiring broadcast journalist Ellen Jones through the lens of three life predictions made by Old Luella, an Alabama soothsayer.

Educating Sadie, published in August 2019, was a finalist in the 2018 William Faulkner – William Wisdom Creative Writing Competition. *Educating Sadie* follows one woman's struggle to help another woman rise above a life of poverty and abuse in the nineteenth-century South. Amanda Oglesby is a first-year teacher who meets Sadie Wiggins, a sharecropper's wife, on the night of the first open house at her new school. Childless, Sadie is drawn to the school: she's bright and wants to learn. The relationship develops further when the new teacher invites Sadie to attend daily classes. A benevolent school board chairman, a beloved boarding house owner, a midwife, a handsome plantation owner, and a misanthrope move in the background of *Educating Sadie,* which gives young readers a portrait of the American South at the turn of the century.

Alayne is a member of the Atlanta Writers Club, the Georgia Association for Instructional Technology, the Georgia Writers Association, the Southeastern Writers Association, and the Society of Children's Book Writers and Illustrators. She currently lives in Lawrenceville, Ga., with her husband.

Made in the USA
Columbia, SC
03 July 2021